LETTERS TO HANNAH

By: Scott Eisenberg

ISBN 978-0692537619 (Untold Stories Publishing, Inc.)

Untold Stories Publishing, Inc.
PO Box 1029
Commack, New York 11725

Cover Design Copyright © 2015
by (http://DigitalDonna.com)

Editing by A Winning Brief, Inc.

This is a work of fiction. Names, characters, businesses, places, events, and incidents are either the products of the author's imagination or used in a fictitious manner. Any resemblance to actual persons, living or dead, or actual events, is purely coincidental.

DEDICATION

To my family. Without whom our perseverance would not have been tested, my struggle would have been lost, and this story would never have been told. I love you. More than words could ever possibly do justice. You saved me, and for that, I am eternally grateful.

And will always handle your legal work *pro bono*.

AUTHOR'S NOTE

I suffer from severe depression. I was first diagnosed with this illness seventeen years ago. Notwithstanding the often devastating effects my illness has had on myself and my loved ones, one of the biggest hurdles for me to get over was writing the previous sentence, and "coming out" to a society which continues to downplay and misconstrue mental illness. **Stigmatization is easier and more cost effective than remedy.**

I have had two significant "episodes" since 1998, with the most recent consuming the better part of 2013 - 2014. I am relieved to say that I made it out alive, stronger than before; and even happier to share this story with you, which was written while in the darkest throes of my depression. I could easily sit and wax poetic about scalpel-happy surgeons, nearly every variety of psychotropic medication, electroconvulsive therapy, and life at some of our country's "most prestigious" mental health facilities.

But to prattle on about all of that would rob you, my new friend, of your right to your own interpretation of my work. If I want to convey anything, it is that there is always a way out. No matter how dark it is, no matter how bleak it appears to be trending, there is always a pathway out. For me, it was mindfulness. For you, it may be something else. But I want you to find that way out, and know that ending your life should never be an option. To do so would only leave things darker for everyone you leave behind.

If you ever experience an urge to harm yourself, I implore you to reach out to someone. A loved one, a friend, a teacher, a mentor. If you truly feel as though you have no

one to talk to, please call the National Suicide Prevention

Lifeline at (800) 273-8255.

CHAPTER I

Kenneth Hill stood at the door of Martin's Funeral

Home greeting mourners as they arrived. His one year old

daughter, Hannah, was at home with a babysitter, being too

young for a service such as this. It had been two days since

Kenneth's wife Frannie had succumbed to cervical cancer after

a relatively brief but brave battle with the disease. The speed

at which the disease had ravaged her body still shocked

Kenneth; it having been two short months since things got

really bad. The chemotherapy and radiation had been ongoing

for quite some time, and Kenneth questioned the effectiveness

of both; he often wondered if she would have been better off

without the treatment. They both seemed to make her sicker,

with the persistent nausea often crippling her more than the disease. She was largely unable to care for their daughter, with that task falling primarily to Kenneth and Kenneth's father.

She did try though. Every night she was home, she read a book to Hannah before putting her in the crib for the night. She performed this ritual no matter her level of nausea. Then she herself would climb back into bed. Kenneth would bring her nightly cocktail of medicines, a rainbow-like assortment of pills, which as far as Kenneth could tell were meant to prolong her suffering, not heal her. He also brought her a cold washcloth to place on her forehead, and would rub her feet until she fell asleep. Although this was usually an effective routine at getting her to fall asleep, it would not last long, as her battle between nausea and sleep would most commonly result in a victory by the former.

It was a brisk fall day when Frannie passed. Fall had

been Frannie's favorite season; she loved to watch the leaves change colors. To hers and Kenneth's dismay, she passed in the hospital as opposed to the comfort of her own home. The doctors knew she had reached the end, and had suggested that they bring Hannah in for her to say goodbye. Amidst a sea of IVs, tubes, and wires, Frannie held Hannah tightly to her chest, alternating between tears and smiles as she kissed her over and over again. "You are going to do great things Princess, always remember that Mommy loves you;" these being her final words to Hannah. Kenneth sat by Frannie as she breathed her last breath; their hands firmly intertwined when he felt her hand go limp. Kenneth kissed her forehead and put his head on her bosom, crying as hard as he could ever remember doing so.

Now, two days later, he could not cry anymore. He simply had no more tears. As he greeted the mourners, the most he could muster was a blank stare. The condolences became repetitive to him and they all began to run together after a while. Once it seemed that everyone was there, Kenneth went back into the family room. In the room were his brother Barry and his wife Michele, his sister Lucy, his father Michael, and his in-laws Larry and Samantha. Kenneth walked over to where Frannie was lying to look upon her one last time. She had a long, natural looking blond wig on, her make-up was done up just as it had been in the picture Kenneth had provided the mortician, and he caught a whiff of her favorite perfume. She looked almost "normal;" however, her illness was belied by her frailty and thinness. It all seemed very artificial to him. Knowing this would be the last time he would ever see her; he again bent down to kiss her on the forehead and placed a photograph of the two of them with Hannah on her chest. He then went with the family into the main congregation room.

The congregation room was filled to capacity, with

some folks standing on the sides. Frannie had been a very well-liked person, having made friends during many activities and in groups such as Gymboree, Toys-for-Tots, baby gymnastics, the United Federation of Teachers, and several different outreach and volunteer groups. She cared a lot for helping people, and she had never been one to turn down an opportunity to do so. They all turned out for the funeral, each person feeling like a piece of them had been lost that day. Kenneth was much different than Frannie on that front, with him preferring to spend his time with his own family after his grueling days at the office. He inwardly lamented that there would only be a fraction of this amount of people at his own funeral someday.

Once the funeral service began, the Rabbi said a number of prayers. He told a story about the physical body being buried in the ground but the "spiritual" body returning home to God, where there would be no more suffering. He then made a number of generic comments about Frannie based upon information that Kenneth had provided him. Next, it was Kenneth's turn to speak. He approached the podium, took out his speech which he had typed up last night, afraid that he would leave something or someone out if he tried to recite a speech from rote memory. There would be no second chances for this speech, and a lot of eyes were on him, not something he was entirely comfortable with. After taking a few deep breaths, he began:

"I thank you all for coming today; it would have warmed Frannie's heart to see such a good turnout. As I look out among all the faces here today, I see both people from Frannie's past and present. More importantly, I see the faces of a lot of people, if not all of you, whose hearts Frannie touched at one time or another. Frannie was a selfless woman who truly cared about others. A lot of people can say they like to help others, but I have found that it is only a small portion of the population who actually do. Frannie fell into the latter group.

By profession, Frannie was a teacher. Having taught second grade for so many years, she was one of the few teachers who had not become jaded by the work and still loved what she did. She touched the lives of hundreds of children over the years. I will never forget the look of pride in her eyes when she finished grading tests, finding that every student had either done well or showed a marked improvement. I will also never forget the time Frannie had a special needs child in her class who was barely capable of spelling his own name, let alone read or write at a grade-appropriate level. His first grade teacher had warned Frannie that he was exceptionally difficult to deal with and that she would have her hands full. Frannie did not look at this as a burden, but instead she rose to the challenge. Instead of simply pushing him through the system, she was determined to get him to come out of his shell and prosper. And sure enough, she succeeded in this goal. By the end of the school year, that same boy was reading and writing at a grade-appropriate level. More importantly, he was also regularly interacting with his peers. Frannie had never been more proud of any of her accomplishments than she was with that. That young boy's parents were eternally grateful for "cracking the shell," and it brings me joy to see them here today to pay their respects to Frannie. She would be overjoyed to see them as well.

Outside of her profession, Frannie was an active member of the community. She was a member of the PTA even though she did not yet have a child in the school system; she simply cared that much about bettering the schools for the children already participating. She was on the Brighton Town Board for several years, another passion of hers, for she genuinely cared about each issue brought before the Board and the opportunity to tackle such issues. She believed that every issue was important, and always acted for the benefit of the Town, never for herself. She valued her selflessness, as did her co-members and constituents. She volunteered her time for countless other groups and associations, never shirking her duties, accomplishing tasks, and invariably making friends along the way. Hence why this is a standing-room only gathering.

Frannie cherished the friends she made, both personally and professionally. She respected everyone equally. Her core group of close friends, her ladies as she called them, meant the world to her. It was a rare Friday night, even after she got sick, that she would miss a "Ladies Night." As far as I understand it, which might require some degree of guesswork since husbands were not permitted to attend or hear about the night, the gals would meet at a local Starbucks or coffee shop and gossip, complain about us, vent their emotions, and occasionally shed a tear. To the ladies, who are all here today, know that Frannie loved each one of you, and your friendship, I believe, played a large role in keeping her going. For that, I thank you.

Now on a more personal level, Frannie was a woman who thrived on the love of her family. She was a wife, a mother, a daughter, a daughter in-law, a sister in-law, an aunt; all roles that she took very seriously. We had dinner every Sunday night, with the whole family being invited. Depending upon what each family member had going on, various members would usually attend. These gatherings, ranging from four to ten people, always perked her up. These dinners continued even after Frannie fell ill, regardless of how nauseous or sick she was from her treatment, she would always encourage us to attend and she would always do so with a smile. She felt that a strong family bond was the cornerstone of a healthy lifestyle. These dinners were always filled with laughter. The one rule, which was implemented by Frannie, was that there was to be no discussion about her illness at the dinners. This again was an act of her selflessness; she wanted to focus to be on upbeat family topics, not the cancer that was eating away at her. And we all happily obliged. Frannie loved every member of her family; they formed her "foundation" as she put it.

This is a perfect segue into a discussion about Hannah. Whereas her family formed her foundation, Hannah was at the core of that foundation. As many of you know, we had some difficulty conceiving a child, which rocked Frannie harder than any illness ever could. After several failed attempts, we were blessed with Hannah. It was hard to believe that there was any incompleteness in Frannie's life, but there was. Frannie was put on this earth to be a mother. When Hannah was born, Frannie became complete. I will never forget the moment Hannah was wrapped in the blanket and handed to Frannie. We all cried together, Frannie called Hannah her "little miracle." From that very moment, Frannie devoted her life to being the best mother possible to our "little miracle." And she succeeded. Never before had I witnessed such nurturing, such unconditional love, as Frannie provided to Hannah. It was simply breathtaking.

After we found out that Frannie had cancer, her first reaction was not at all about her fate. Again, selfless. Her first reaction was to lament how Hannah was going to grow up without a mother. She was absolutely distraught at that thought. The only saving grace, according to Frannie, was that Hannah would be too young to remember her mother's illness, and would not have to witness the deterioration of her body. Frannie did everything possible to make her brief time with Hannah pleasurable and memorable. She never let her disease get in the way, regardless of how sick she was. Almost up until the very end, before Frannie left for the hospital for the final time, she fed Hannah every night, read her a story even though she was too young to appreciate them, and rocked her to sleep. She would then kiss her goodnight and put her in the bassinet or the crib. It was a truly beautiful sight to see. Hannah was her heart, her guiding light, for almost a year, and Frannie soaked up every minute of it. Every person here can learn something about true love if you just stop and think about the relationship between Hannah and Frannie.

Frannie was my everything. She was my wife, my best friend, my lover, my confidant, my guru. She was simply my girl. We were together for fifteen years and married for nine years. We did everything with each other, as a team. There was a bond between us that was unshakeable, and certainly withstood the test of time. I always admired Frannie, but never more than I did these past twelve months. During these past twelve months, I learned from her what it meant to be strong, what it meant to be brave, what it meant to be resilient,

- 13 -

what it meant to be a fighter, and what it meant to love

unconditionally. For that, I will be forever grateful and will

forever honor and love her.

Goodbye my love, may you rest easy now knowing

that I will devote my life to raising Hannah with the same

morals and values as you would have instilled in her. You will

never be forgotten, I love you with all my heart."

And with that, Kenneth faced Frannie's coffin and held

his hand to his heart, saying "I love you" so faintly that only

he could hear it. The Rabbi finished the service, and then

everyone, Kenneth included, headed to their cars, with the

cemetery as their intended destination. There, Kenneth would

say his final goodbye, and then assume fully the role as a

single parent to Hannah, a role Kenneth promised Frannie he

would devote his life to.

CHAPTER II

Jennifer Daniels's day started out as a normal one. She awoke at 6:00 am after a good night's sleep. She took a little extra time in the shower, figuring she could make up the time on the back end of her morning routine. She was a creature of habit if nothing else.

Jennifer was twenty-nine years old, never married. She had a few failed relationships along the way, usually failing because she valued her independence, what her mother called her isolation, too much. Commitment was not something that came naturally to her. To the contrary, she learned from a very young age that commitment was not a right, but a privilege that could be stripped away.

Jennifer grew up without a father, hers having abandoned her and her mother when she was two years old. She had not seen or heard from him in twenty-seven years, having given up hope for a "Hallmark" reunion a long time ago. With her mother holding down two jobs to support them, Jennifer developed a strong sense of independence and abandonment at a very young age.

At seventeen, she enrolled in a local community college, mostly to appease her mother. Her grades were average; she did the bare minimum just to get by. She did not care much about school, her aspirations for greatness never having taken off the ground.

During college, she worked part-time at the local post office. The money wasn't much, but Jennifer did not have any extravagant vices that necessitated much money. The job also did not require too much in the way of creative thinking. Her role was limited to sorting the incoming mail into the proper bins. On occasion, if the post office was short-staffed, she would be called upon to work the front counter. This was welcomed with discontent, as social interaction of any kind filled her with anxiety. She did not need any type of psychoanalysis to tell her she suffered from, at the very least, a long-standing social disorder.

After graduating college, Jennifer switched to full-time at the post office. Much to the chagrin of her mother, she decided not to pursue a career that would utilize the degree in communications she had just earned. Granted, her mother had no idea what one does with a communications degree, but she was fairly certain it involved more than working at the post office.

It was just a normal day when the first letter to Hannah arrived.

CHAPTER III

Kenneth Hill sat in the shower sobbing uncontrollably.

It had been two months since his beloved daughter Hannah

was taken from him, fifty-six days since he had buried her

tiny body in the ground. Hannah had been only five years old,

and had been raised solely by her father after her mother,

Frannie, had died of cervical cancer.

It was a rainy Saturday evening when Kenneth and

Hannah were returning home from an early movie. They had

gone to see *Frozen* twice already, but Hannah insisted on

seeing it again. Kenneth, by profession was a tough

negotiator, but had not won an argument with Hannah since

she started talking. To say he was wrapped around her

miniscule fingers is akin to saying that Hitler was a bit of a grump.

They were driving along Birch Street, as they had done a million times before, while the two of them sang "Let it Go" together. Kenneth never saw the other car coming. As they crossed the intersection of Birch and Elm Street, an SUV driven by an intoxicated teenager blew through a red light and hit the passenger side of Kenneth's vehicle. Kenneth was unharmed, as was the other driver.

A well-meaning EMT told Kenneth that Hannah had died upon impact. This was not a consolation of any sort. In the blink of an eye, his world was shattered, his heart ripped from his body.

The next few days were a complete whirlwind, a blur of friends and family coming and going. If he never heard "it was all a part of God's plan" again, it would be too soon. Words were meaningless. It had been like a dark shroud had been pulled down over Kenneth's eyes, forever plunging his world into a hazy shade of darkness.

At the urging of his sister Lucy, Kenneth began immediately seeing a therapist on a weekly basis. He was hesitant at first, but at least had the sensibility to recognize that he needed help. He was not going to be able to navigate the waters of grief by himself. It was the therapist who suggested that Kenneth try to express his grief by writing letters to Hannah; it was Kenneth's own idea to actually mail them.

CHAPTER IV

Jennifer clocked in at 9:00 am sharp, punctuality always being a staple of her personality. She exchanged the obligatory pleasantries with her co-workers Sam and Louis. Both Sam and Louis had been working at the post office as long as Jennifer had, and they represented the closest people she would refer to as "friends."

Sam had started working at the post office at around the same time as Jennifer and was fairly close in age. He was Jennifer's polar opposite, being one who loved and thrived off of social interactions. It had taken Sam a long time to crack Jennifer's "outer shell "to a point where she would interact with him. Even if it was just a "hello, how are you," this was a big step for Jennifer. She liked Sam, or did not mind him at least, and on occasion would engage him in conversation.

Louis was much older than Sam and Jennifer, sort of the elder statesman of the post office. He had been working at that same branch office much longer than the other two, regularly bemoaning the fact that stamps used to cost a quarter. Louis would converse with Sam more than he would with Jennifer, a fact that Jennifer had come to appreciate. It wasn't that she did not like Louis, she just found his attempts at conversation with her annoying and intrusive. Louis felt his intentions were friendly, but he learned a long time ago that Jennifer was apathetic to his efforts and adjusted accordingly.

Once the post office opened, Sam and Louis took their positions at the front counter, ready to face the morning rush of traffic. Out of sight in the back was Jennifer, diligently sorting the incoming mail.

Receiving unaddressed mail was nothing new to

Jennifer. The post office received hundreds of such pieces of mail per year, usually addressed to God, Santa Claus, the Easter Bunny, and the Tooth Fairy. These pieces of mail would always be returned to the sender stamped "Undeliverable: Address Unknown." Jennifer could not say what made this letter stand out, or what prompted her to take it home with her that day in direct violation of post office regulations and federal law. The letter came addressed to "Hannah Hill, Heaven." According to the return address, the letter had come from Kenneth Hill at an address located in Brighton, the same town as the post office.

Jennifer put the letter to the side, inexplicably disregarding the post office's regulation to process unaddressed mail as undeliverable. She continued her task of sorting the incoming mail, not being able to take her mind off of that single, unaddressed letter. The rest of her shift was kind of a blur as she eagerly awaited the day's end so she could get home.

At 4:00 pm, Jennifer clocked out and left the post office with the letter secretly tucked into her purse. This was a flagrant breach of post office rules, but for some reason Jennifer did not think twice about doing it. There was something drawing her to this particular letter that made her overlook the rule for the first time in her tenure there.

Jennifer was a creature of routine and upon her arrival at her apartment that routine always began with a warm greeting from her cat, Binky. Jennifer did not have any friends, perhaps outside of Sam, so Binky provided her with her sole source of companionship. Normally she would head straight into the kitchen and throw a Lean Cuisine in the microwave and go get changed out of her work clothes while it heated up. Once done, she would take her meal with a glass of wine and sit in the living room with Binky for the remainder of the night, television on. She may have been alone, but she never felt lonely.

Tonight, however, was different. She eschewed her normal routine, much to the chagrin of Binky, for the opportunity to read the letter she had taken. After taking her shoes off, she took the letter and placed it on the living room table facing her as she sat on the couch. She spent a few minutes just staring at it, reassuring herself that opening it and reading it was the right thing to do. She stared at the words again, saying them out loud as if such vocalization would provide her the answer. "Hannah Hill, Heaven," over and over again, until she finally found the courage to open it.

Upon opening the envelope, Jennifer found multiple loose leaf pages folded neatly into a rectangle, along with a photograph of a man and a little girl sharing cotton candy. The man appeared to be in his late 30s and the girl could not have been more than five or six years old. She was a beautiful little girl, with long, flowing blond hair, blue eyes, and a smile that seemed to jump right out of the photograph. She

presumed, already feeling her heart ache, that the little girl

was Hannah and the man was Kenneth Hill. Without wasting

any more time, Jennifer unfolded the paper, sat back on the

couch, and began to read.

September 23, 2014

My Dearest Hannah,

It has been two months since you were taken from me,

since my heart was unapologetically ripped from my chest. I

am trying so hard to process what happened, but I simply am

unable to wrap my mind around it. You were only five-years-

old, you had your whole life ahead of you. You used to love

looking at pictures of Mommy from before she got sick, you

always said how beautiful she was. When Mommy got sick

and died a few years ago, it was you, even if you were too

young to know it, who got me through that time. You lifted

me up and showed me that I could still express and receive love. You showed me joy, you showed me freedom. Freedom from a darkness that had enveloped me.

Now, once again, my life is shrouded in darkness. I can still hear your laughter, your uncontrollable laughter when you were visited by the tickle monster, and envision your radiant smile when you saw butterflies flying around you. Oh how you loved butterflies. I miss looking at rainbows together; you were always so amazed by the brightness of the colors.

I can still picture you on your first day of kindergarten, with your *Frozen* backpack, waiting for the bus. You held my hand so tightly as we waited for the bus, afraid of the new challenge ahead of you. But you rose to the challenge and had a great first day. I had no doubt you would rise to the challenge as you were the strongest person I knew. I gained my strength from you. Now, I have no source of strength. I am depleted.

My doctor suggested that I write you letters as a way to help me heal, believing this would be a good medium to communicate my feelings. I am unsure of this, for it hurts so much. I will continue to write the letters, however, as I simply need to do something. Anything.

I enclosed the picture of you and me eating cotton candy after leaving the circus. That was such a joyous occasion for me. Do you remember how silly the man who took the picture thought we were? Your tongue was all blue from the cotton candy, it was so much fun stuffing it in each other's mouths.

Hannah, my princess, I miss you more than I know how to express. I hope that you are experiencing nothing but joy and happiness wherever you are, and maybe you can figure out how to send some my way. I love you now, always, and forever.

Love,
Daddy

As the tears streamed down her face, Jennifer read and re-read the letter two more times. While she was able to glean certain facts from the letter herself, she was determined to find out all she could about Hannah.

CHAPTER V

Jennifer vaguely recalled something in the news from a few months back about a little girl who was killed in a car accident.

Opening up her laptop, she typed "Hannah, car accident, Brighton" into Google. There was no shortage of results. A man named Kenneth Hill was driving with his five year old daughter home from the movies when their car was broadsided by another car driven by a drunk driver. Kenneth and the other driver were unharmed. However, Hannah, who was fastened securely in her car seat, was killed upon impact. The other driver was arrested and charged with vehicular manslaughter, among other crimes, and is expected to spend the next several decades in prison. To Kenneth, that was no justice at all.

After reading several more news articles, Jennifer closed up the apartment and got ready for bed. She climbed into bed next to Binky, who was already snuggled up on Jennifer's pillow, and spent the next two hours thinking about Hannah and Kenneth. Having a full understanding now of how Hannah's life had been robbed of her at such a young age, and having read Kenneth's letter, she simply could not fall asleep.

She could not explain the feeling, but she felt compelled to act. The problem was that she did not know what to do. She thought about seeking out and approaching Kenneth Hill. What would she even say to him? After carefully considering this option, she decided that it could only do more harm than good. As she thought about what to do, she slowly drifted off to sleep.

Around 3:00 am, Jennifer awoke with a start. She did not know where the idea came from, but it was significant enough to wake her up from a dead sleep. As she put on her slippers and robe, Binky, who was obviously not impressed with the timing of Jennifer's revelation, barely stirred from her sleep.

Jennifer went into the kitchen, put the lights on, and made herself a cup of hot chocolate in her Keurig machine, one of her few, allotted extravagances. Jennifer had never been a coffee drinker, notwithstanding that her mother had been an avid coffee drinker in the house as Jennifer grew up. She sat down and read Kenneth's letter again. Rereading Kenneth's letter again reaffirmed for Jennifer that it deserved a response, and the best way to do so would be to write a letter back to him. The caveat, she concluded, was that the letter would come from Hannah, not Jennifer. If the idea did not work, she assumed she would simply not receive any further letters from him. However, if it was successful, she believed she could provide some relief, perhaps even some joy to Kenneth.

So with that in mind, she opened up a spiral notebook and began to write.

September 29, 2014

Dear Daddy,

I was <u>so</u> <u>so</u> <u>so</u> happy to get your letter. I have so much to tell you. When I got here, I found Mommy right away. She was so excited to see me, although she did tell me it was way too soon. She is really beautiful, and she said I look just like her. I am very happy she found me so quickly, especially because she helped me read your letter, there were a lot of words that I did not understand. She also helped me a lot to write this letter back to you.

I know you told me that Mommy left us when I was

very young because she got sick, but I want you to know that she is not sick anymore. She looks just like she did in the pictures you showed me. She has long, beautiful blond hair and bright blue eyes, just like the blue in the rainbows we used to look at together.

Daddy, even though I was happy to get your letter, it made me sad to know that you are so sad. You must be very lonely with both me and Mommy gone, but I want you to be happy. I am not in any kind of pain and neither is Mommy. We are very happy here together. The people here are really nice and there are a lot of kids my age to play with. Me and Mommy play a lot together and she cannot stop hugging and kissing me all the time.

You said in your letter that you live in darkness and that made me really sad. I want your life to be filled with light. I asked the people here if they could shine some light on you so you would not be in the darkness all the time, but they said only you could bring yourself out of the darkness. I was not really sure what they meant by that.

I want you to be happy Daddy, and so does Mommy. It would be great if you wrote me another letter, I will also write you back. I drew you a picture and put it into this envelope, do you like it? It is a picture of me and Mommy, I hope you like it.

That is all I can think of right now. I miss you THIS MUCH and I love you even more.

Love,
Your Princess Hannah

Jennifer felt very confident about the letter and felt that Kenneth would certainly get joy out of reading it. The next day, she brought it with her to work and mailed it, again feeling very good about herself.

CHAPTER VI

Kenneth Hill's day started out like any other since he

lost Hannah. To say he woke up is not entirely accurate as he

never really slept, drifting somewhere between reality and

nightmare. Good REM sleep had eluded him, and his daily

demeanor was more akin to a zombie than a human. He had

very little appetite and had lost a considerable amount of

weight, with bourbon comprising the majority of his daily

caloric intake. He stopped going to the gym. It was a rare

occasion when he left the house; such occasions were limited

to the bare necessities: the grocery store, the liquor store, or

the pharmacy to refill any of the numerous psychosomatic

drugs he was now on. These pills, a rainbow-like assortment of colors, were supposed to make him feel "better," as if a set of pills could compensate for the piece of his heart that was missing.

He had not been back to work in nearly three months. As an attorney, missing even a single day could negatively impact one's workload and ever-present billable hour requirement, so he could not imagine, nor did he try, to understand how the firm was handling his absence. He truly could not bring himself to care. The "powers that be" at the firm had told him he could take as long as he needed; however, he was realistic enough to know that this generosity was going to have a shelf life. What that shelf life was he did not know, nor did he care enough to inquire. At this point, the concept of work was nothing but foreign to him, with him barely having enough concentration to watch a commercial on television.

His family was concerned for him. His father lived nearby, and if it were up to him, he would be over his house every day. Kenneth could not handle that frequency of consolation, as it was not something he found helpful. He also had two siblings, Barry and Lucy, who checked in on him periodically, usually by text. Phone calls or actual visits did not entirely fit in with their "hectic" schedules. His relationships with his friends had also become strained, not through any fault of theirs. They called regularly, offered to come over and cook for him, offered to take him out. However, Kenneth rejected all of these efforts. It's not that he was unappreciative of the efforts, he simply could not bring himself to accept the goodwill. He was a shell of his former self, a shell that he was simply waiting to crack apart at any given time.

It was an idle Tuesday when his otherwise dark life was changed forever. He had just forced down some turkey breast when he heard the sound of his mailbox open and close. Similarly finding mail uninteresting, he made no rush to retrieve it. Instead, he went back into his bedroom where he laid in darkness for several hours. He did not sleep at all, he just lay in bed with the shades drawn and blankets covering his head. This was his new temple. There he cried for hours on end.

Thoughts of suicide came and went, oftentimes he just could not see the point in going on. On one hand, he felt that taking his own life would lead to a reunion with both his wife and his daughter. On the other hand, he had heard somewhere along the way that committing suicide was a "sin" and would not lead him on the path to his girls. He was not a religious person, but he did not, at that time, want to press his luck. However, knowing that someday his emotions might get the best of him and he would succumb, he made sure that all his loose ends were tied up. Whatever money he had saved up was left in trust for his niece Stacey and his nephew Alex, both

his brother Barry's children. He left his house to his brother

and sister, assuming they could sell it for a handsome profit to

be divided between them. That is all there was as far as assets.

He had tried several times, albeit unsuccessfully, to write a

suicide letter. He finally gave up that endeavor, figuring

people would simply understand.

Kenneth got out of bed after spending almost three

hours hiding from the world, somewhat fulfilling his goal of

passing time until he could medicate himself with a sufficient

amount of bourbon and Klonopin to put him to sleep for the

night. He begrudgingly took a hot shower, which he found

calming enough to warrant his staying in there for almost an

hour. This had essentially become his daily routine, one he

half-jokingly referred to as his "non-existent existence."

After his shower, he threw on a pair of sweatpants and

a tee shirt, and headed downstairs to retrieve the mail. He

brought the mail into the kitchen and tossed it down on the kitchen table. Assuming it was the normal stack of bills and junk mail, he initially paid no attention to it. However, something caught his eye that stopped him dead in his tracks. Tucked in among the rest of the mail was a letter addressed to "Daddy," with a return address of "Hannah Hill, Heaven." Astonished, he nearly collapsed on the floor. He picked up the letter and read and re-read the return address over and over again, completely baffled.

He placed the letter down on the kitchen table, too scared at the moment to open it. He poured himself a glass of bourbon and drank it down in one gulp. He poured himself another glass and brought it along with the letter to the living room. He had to put all the lights on because he had gotten in the habit of keeping all lights in the house off unless he specifically needed them. He preferred the darkness.

Now that he was swashed in light, he sat with his

bourbon, and the envelope on the table in front of him. After working up enough courage to open the envelope, he pulled out several pages of what seemed to be a handwritten letter and hand drawn picture. He took a big gulp of bourbon and began to read the letter.

After finishing the letter, Kenneth looked at the picture Hannah had drawn. It was a picture of Hannah and his wife, Frannie, holding hands, with a bright rainbow behind them and tons of butterflies. Hannah loved butterflies. Frannie had a pink nose, and this made Kenneth laugh. This occurrence shocked him, once he realized he was actually laughing, for it had been more than two months since he had done so.

It was a while before he got up from the couch. He read and reread the letter numerous times, a sense of warmth overcoming him. This was not just the bourbon. Reading Hannah's words brought upon him a sort of sense of worth, something that had also eluded him for a long time. He finally got up and got ready to go to sleep. He was determined to

maintain and prolong this "heavenly pen pal ship," and he felt

a newfound sense of purpose. That night, he slept better than

he had in months.

CHAPTER VII

The next day, Kenneth awoke after his first, good night's sleep in months feeling alive. He had a 10:00 am appointment with his therapist, Dr. Kaplan, whom he began seeing shortly after Hannah died at the behest of his family. Thus far, he had a difficult time saying if the therapy was helping him or not. The problem, as Kenneth saw it, was that he did not want to ever "get over" Hannah's death or "put it behind him," which seemed somewhat contradictory to what Dr. Kaplan was encouraging him to do. Learning to manage his grief was also a goal of Dr. Kaplan's, one which was more palatable to Kenneth.

He arrived at Dr. Kaplan's office a few minutes early,

this having been his first excursion out of the house in four days. Dr. Kaplan's office was a bit outdated, the waiting room being filled with furnishings that looked like they were ripped from the pages of a 1980s furniture catalog.

The furnishings were not the only things that seemed antiquated, Dr. Kaplan himself seemed a bit so as well. He was well into his 70s, and often spoke about his training with "notable" psychologists that Kenneth had never heard of, and whom he assumed had long since passed on. Not that Dr. Kaplan was bad at what he did, far from it, it just seemed like he may not have updated his treatment techniques in quite some time. He had, however, come highly recommended by several people, so Kenneth was willing to put forth the effort with the treatment for now.

The meeting started as they all do, with Dr. Kaplan asking how his previous week had been. Kenneth did not share the receipt of Hannah's letter at first because he was scared at how it would be received by Dr. Kaplan. He told Dr. Kaplan that the previous week had been awful, on par with all of the previous weeks he had been in treatment. He had not left the house, he had not shaved, barely eaten, avoided phone calls, and generally avoided social contact with anyone altogether. Dr. Kaplan responded in kind by advising Kenneth that such behaviors were counterproductive towards his healing. Kenneth responded by saying that none of these activities would bring Hannah back to him, nor would they make the pain go away. They had essentially reached a stalemate in Kenneth's eyes, so Kenneth decided that this would be as good a time as any to bring up the letters.

He advised Dr. Kaplan that he had taken the doctor's advice and wrote Hannah a letter, but further advised him that he had taken it one step further and mailed it to Hannah in Heaven. Dr. Kaplan, taken aback by this information, initially had mixed feelings about Kenneth's course of action.

He was pleased that Kenneth had written the letter, as he found over the years that this was a tremendous help to those engaging in loss therapy. It generally provided a strong medium to express thoughts, feelings, and emotions that the writer otherwise did not have an outlet for. As far as mailing the letter, Dr. Kaplan expressed some concern over the possible and likely eventual disappointment of simply receiving the letter back from the post office as undeliverable. Dr. Kaplan felt that this was also counterproductive as Kenneth would be faced with the reality that no one was reading his letter. This could lead Kenneth to step backwards and stop writing altogether, thus defeating the purpose of the exercise.

It was at this moment that Kenneth told Dr. Kaplan that he received a response from Hannah. At first, Dr. Kaplan was speechless, not something that had happened to him during his forty-five years of practicing psychology. He recognized immediately that he had to tread carefully, for this was a very sensitive development. He also recognized that this would explain Kenneth's slightly improved demeanor, what Dr. Kaplan referred to in his notes as an "altered jubilation, restrained joy."

Indulging Kenneth, Dr. Kaplan asked what "Hannah" had written to him in the letter. Kenneth described its contents almost verbatim, as he had read the letter so many times it was nearly committed to memory. He explained that Hannah had met up with her deceased mother, described what she looked like, and advised that neither her mother nor her were in any kind of physical pain. After asking Kenneth what he originally wrote to Hannah, it became apparent to Dr. Kaplan that "Hannah" had only written about information that could have been gleaned from Kenneth's letter, confirming his suspicion that a would be do-gooder had read Kenneth's letter and responded accordingly. The question was why.

On the one hand, the letter's response could be viewed as a good thing, as this was the most upbeat Dr. Kaplan had seen Kenneth since Hannah passed. It appeared to give him a sense of purpose which Dr. Kaplan had not seen before. However, there was an enormous sense of disappointment and emptiness that Kenneth could be setting himself up for if this unknown person decided to stop writing. Dr. Kaplan explained this, very gently, to Kenneth; unfortunately, Kenneth was not grasping this.

Dr. Kaplan's fear was confirmed. Kenneth was under the impression that this letter had actually come from Hannah. Although Kenneth was a highly educated, highly intelligent man, he seemed to have developed a strong disconnect between reality and fantasy. This concerned Dr. Kaplan greatly, believing that this was a tremendous setback for Kenneth, and a very negative development in Kenneth's progress. Their time together for the day came to an end, so

Dr. Kaplan decided to table the topic until the next appointment. While Dr. Kaplan was concerned, Kenneth left the meeting still riding the high of this new development, eager to write back to Hannah.

CHAPTER VIII

Kenneth sat down with his usual glass of bourbon at the kitchen table, pen and paper in hand. He felt a sufficient amount of time had passed before writing Hannah back. He had so much to share.

November 11, 2014

My Dearest Hannah,

What a wonderful surprise it was to receive your letter and picture. I LOVED the picture, I thought it was very funny that you gave Mommy a pink nose. I would like to draw you a picture, but as you know, I cannot draw very well. Do you remember that time I tried to draw you a picture of a dog? It looked like a hot dog with wheels! You laughed and laughed so hard, I can still hear you laughing. It was the most beautiful sound. There was never a sound that warmed my heart as much as your laughter.

I am very happy that Mommy found you and is there for you to spend time with. Isn't she beautiful? Do you remember when I showed you our wedding picture? She made the most beautiful bride. Her blond hair flowed so smoothly and her eyes were as blue as the sky, just like yours. It warms my heart to hear that she is not sick anymore, and it also warms my heart to hear that you are not in any kind of pain.

I am glad that there are children there for you to play with. What types of games do you play? Have you made any good friends? I am sure you have, you always were good at making new friends. What types of things do you do with Mommy?

I am sorry that I expressed to you how sad I am. But I wanted to be honest with you, and I thought it might help me to tell you that. To be honest, I never thought you would receive or read my letter. But I am very sad that you are not here with me, I miss you so much. I miss your voice, your laugh, your beautiful face. I miss putting you to bed every night, wishing you pretty princess dreams and hearing you wish me pretty king dreams in return. You did not like thunder storms, and would call me into your room when they were happening. I would lie down next to you and you would snuggle up against me, and we would fall asleep together, listening to the rain. Every time thunder struck, I would feel you squeeze me a little tighter.

I always was there to protect you. But on that night coming back from the movies, I was not able to do so. I could not stop you from getting hurt, and I am having a hard time living with that fact. I failed you. I hope that you can forgive me for that. I love you Princess, always and forever.

Love,
Daddy

CHAPTER IX

Jennifer read Kenneth's latest letter and had very mixed

emotions. She felt horrible that Kenneth blamed himself for

Hannah's death; from everything she had read, it was

Kenneth's vehicle that had been struck by a drunk driver.

There was nothing he could have done differently that would

have avoided the accident and his losing Hannah. She felt

compelled to get this across to him somehow.

His latest letter did, as a whole, seem to be more upbeat

than his previous one. This was a positive development, and

one that Jennifer was encouraged by. It had become her goal,

one could even call it a mission, to try and help Kenneth with

his grieving process and to live a meaningful life, if such a life was still possible for him. For better or for worse, it had actually become her sole goal in life. The possibility of receiving letters from Kenneth had become her driving force in life, and the first thought in her mind when she awoke every morning.

She shared this fact and her letter writing campaign with her mother. To say that her mother disapproved was an understatement. She told Jennifer that if that truly was her driving force in life, than she was living a very empty existence. Jennifer's mother was downright worried about both Jennifer and Kenneth, the latter of whom she had never met and knew nothing about. Jennifer's mother had been a mental health counselor, so she had been trained in diagnosing and treating emotional disorders. She expressed her opinion that Jennifer was suffering from a growing case of depression and social anxiety, and that the letter writing was only going to make matters worse. She advised that not only was it going to cause a marked decline in Jennifer's conditions, but could prove to be downright harmful to Kenneth. It was creating a false sense of hope for him, and if and when she stopped writing, he would be crushed beyond repair. She also expressed concern that Jennifer had no friends and never left her apartment except to go to work.

These were the exact reasons why Jennifer chose not to see or speak to her mother very often. For as long as she could remember, her mother had been trying to diagnose her with various emotional disorders. Nothing Jennifer ever did was good enough; it seemed to her that her entire life had been put under a microscope. Jennifer felt that her mother was confusing depression with isolation, the latter of which was Jennifer's personal choice and preference. She did not feel she was depressed, nor did she equate isolation with depression or social anxiety. She could interact with others, she just chose not to. Besides, she had Binky, whom her mother referred to as a "poor substitute" for human contact. Jennifer disagreed, and unsurprisingly, felt that Binky's presence was the only real contact she needed in this world.

Jennifer's mother had been trying to tag her with the "depression label" since she was a young girl. When she was six years old, her mother sent her for pre-adolescent counseling with Dr. Arlovski, a "noted" child psychologist because Jennifer did not have any friends and seemed to prefer solitude to making new friends, or any friends for that matter. Jennifer resented that she had to go to see this doctor when there was nothing wrong with her. The sessions were generally fruitless, with Dr. Arlovski doing the majority of the talking while Jennifer sat there in a "non-communicative state." She did not like Dr. Arlovski; he stunk of cigarettes and constantly asked her the same questions over and over again. "Why don't you like making friends? How does being alone all the time make you feel? Don't you think it would be fun to have friends to play with?" She typically would not respond to these inquiries, mainly because she found the topics to be on the boring side. She also did not necessarily know the answers to these questions; she just preferred to be by herself.

Dr. Arlovski explained to Jennifer's mother that Jennifer showed signs of anti-social behavior, in addition to early signs of depression. Against Dr. Arlovski's recommendation, Jennifer was not put on any medications. Thankfully for Jennifer, her mother did not believe in putting children on psychotropic medications. However, her mother had recently begun to question whether this had been the right decision given Jennifer's current condition. Jennifer stopped seeing Dr. Arlovski when she turned seven, completing no more than eight sessions with him. Her mother felt that given her training, she would be able to treat Jennifer as needed.

So now, some twenty-two years later, Jennifer sat

across from her mother in the living room of her childhood home. Her mother asked if she could see Kenneth's letters, a request which Jennifer vehemently opposed. She cherished the relationship she had developed with Kenneth and wanted it completely guarded from her mother's unrelenting microscope. Her mother asked how work was, to which Jennifer responded that "it was fine." Her mother then asked the inevitable follow-up question: "when are you going to leave that dead-end job and utilize your college degree to do something meaningful?" This was usually the point the visit would come to an end, and today was no different. Jennifer could not stand having her lifestyle questioned by her mother, feeling that her life was trudging along exactly as she wanted it to. And she felt that her new pen pal ship only heightened that experience.

Jennifer left her mother's house shortly thereafter, swallowing her usual sense of agitation and disappointment at the fact that the two of them could not have a "normal" visit. In Jennifer's eyes, a "normal" visit would be one where her life choices were not questioned, and her psyche was not habitually criticized. She gave up hope on this issue a long time ago, however. Onwards.

CHAPTER X

Kenneth sat across from Dr. Kaplan for his weekly

session, somewhat defensive almost from the get-go. Dr.

Kaplan, just like Jennifer's mother, asked if he could read the

letters that he had received from Hannah. Kenneth replied in

the negative, he felt they were too personal. Dr. Kaplan asked

Kenneth very pointedly whether he knew that the letters were

not actually coming from Hannah. Kenneth pointed to specific

comments that Hannah wrote about that no person could

have known. Dr. Kaplan asked if a stranger could be gleaning

information from his letters and responding accordingly.

Kenneth did not want to hear any of this and for the first time

since he began treating with Dr. Kaplan, he got up and walked out.

Dr. Kaplan spent the remainder of Kenneth's allotted time slot writing copious notes about Kenneth. He felt that Kenneth had completely disassociated himself from reality, and was very much in danger of a full psychotic break. He grappled internally with this development because he felt partially responsible. When he first suggested that Kenneth write letters, he had no thoughts that the suggestion would backfire so fiercely. He never had suggested that Kenneth mail the letters, he wanted the letters to function more as a journal. Perhaps he should have been clearer, but this was moot at this point.

Dr. Kaplan was not too proud to admit when he needed help, and this was one of those times. He placed a call to his long-time friend and colleague, Dr. Ellis. He had known Dr. Ellis for more than fifty years, both having earned their doctorate degrees at the same time and at the same schools.

Dr. Ellis was one of the smartest men he had ever met, and certainly one of the most prominent and capable psychologists in the northeast.

When Dr. Ellis called him back, the two men exchanged pleasantries and caught up a bit before Dr. Kaplan explained Kenneth's situation in full detail. Dr. Ellis remembered reading the story in the newspaper about Kenneth's accident and Hannah's passing, but had not known that Kenneth was treating with Dr. Kaplan. Dr. Ellis was not shy in telling Dr. Kaplan that the letter writing campaign was not a good idea. The potential negatives, as Dr. Kaplan had failed to recognize, far outweighed any potential gains.

Dr. Kaplan explained how Kenneth really seemed to believe that he was receiving letters from Hannah. Dr. Ellis was greatly troubled by this and reiterated that such an illogical response was not at all surprising given Kenneth's fragile state. He was somewhat surprised at the way Dr.

Kaplan treated Kenneth. While Dr. Kaplan could not have foreseen Kenneth's act of mailing the letters or his receiving "responses," Dr. Ellis felt it had been an irresponsible treatment plan. He recommended to Dr. Kaplan that he urge Kenneth to stop writing immediately. Dr. Kaplan opined that it was too late and he would not be able to convince Kenneth to stop. Dr. Kaplan admitted that he was at a bit of a loss, a sentiment to which Dr. Ellis did not know how to respond. He advised Dr. Kaplan that he would give the problem some thought and get back to him. Dr. Kaplan hung up the phone, feeling even more helpless than before.

CHAPTER XI

Jennifer walked to work, a little anxious about the day ahead of her. She casually greeted Sam and Louis and took her spot by the incoming mail bin to start her sorting for the day. During her lunch break, she uncharacteristically asked Sam if he wanted to eat with her. She had made the decision to share what she had been doing with Hannah's letters with Sam, mainly for selfish reasons. On occasion, Sam would handle the sorting of incoming mail if Jennifer was out or Louis needed her help up front. Jennifer wanted to ensure that if any letters to Hannah came through, he did not put them in the undeliverable bin and instead put them aside for her.

She of course was hesitant, mainly because what she

was doing was not only against post office regulations but was also a violation of federal law. She had known Sam for a long time and trusted him. They walked to a local sandwich shop for convenience sake, neither of them having ever eaten there before. Jennifer was not really hungry so she ordered only a salad, Sam ordered a sandwich. They sat down at a table in the corner, Jennifer hoping for a modicum of privacy for what she had to share.

"I asked you to lunch because I wanted to share something with you. It is going to seem somewhat surprising and I need you to promise not to tell anyone what I am about to tell you." Jennifer began the conversation.

"You asking me to lunch was the most surprising thing I have experienced in a long time, so it will be tough to top that," Sam replied.

"A few months ago, I started taking certain pieces of mail from work."

"What? Why? And why are you telling me this?"

"It is not mail that had to be delivered. It is mail that would have been returned to the sender as undeliverable."

"You realize that does not make it any better right? Do you understand what would happen if Louis found out?"

"I know it does not make a difference and yes I realize Louis cannot find out. That is why I came to you. Let me explain."

And with that intro, Jennifer described in detail Kenneth and Hannah's story, how Hannah's life had been taken, how she received Kenneth's first letter, and the pen pal ship that had developed since. She left out no details.

Sam was left speechless at first. He had known Jennifer for many years and this seemed so out of character for her. She was one of the most shy, most introverted, and anti-social people he had ever met. He finally processed what had just been told to him and asked: "What are you hoping to accomplish by writing this man?"

"My goal was to bring some closure to Kenneth, maybe even some joy. The part of my plan that was admittedly not thought out very well was that once I started, stopping at any point in time would likely crush Kenneth all over again." Ironically, this was Dr. Kaplan's fear as well. "I thought I was doing a good deed, I did not quite expect it to pan out the way it has," Jennifer continued.

"If I may be frank, it does not sound like you thought this through at all."

"Ok, I did not share this with you so you could pass judgment on me. If I may also be frank, your opinions of my action mean very little to me." Part of Jennifer's charm was her ability to make other people feel entirely worthless.

"So then why are you telling me all this?" Sam asked.

"Because I need your help ensuring that I get all of Kenneth's letters. There are times when you are sorting the incoming mail, and I want you to put Kenneth's letters aside if you receive any. They are always addressed to "Hannah Hill, Heaven" with a return address of "Kenneth Hill, Brighton."

"So you essentially invited me to lunch to ask me to break the law and risk getting fired?"

"Just skirting the law, not breaking it." I'm not asking you to open any of the letters."

"Do you think you can win me over with semantics?"

"You may not ever be in a position to have to do this for me, so all this may be moot."

"You are asking a lot of me Jennifer. Especially since this is the most you have ever said to me in one sitting." After careful consideration, Sam continued: "fine, I will do it. But you have to do me a favor."

"What?"

"Do not tell this story to anyone else. A - I do not want to get in to trouble. B - you sound fucking nuts."

"Fine on both points. Thank you."

And with that having been the longest conversation they had ever had, they finished the remainder of their lunch in silence. Once finished, they walked back to the post office, also in complete silence.

Jennifer felt good having shared her story with Sam, at least feeling a bit more confident that she would not miss any of Kenneth's letters.

CHAPTER XII

That night, Jennifer arrived home at around 6:00 pm, set to write a return letter to Kenneth. She first had her traditional Lean Cuisine for dinner and paid some attention to Binky. She felt bad but she had all but neglected her furry feline friend recently, her mind being too focused on other things. Before setting out to write her letter, she re-read Kenneth's most recent letter to make sure she answered what was asked and responded appropriately.

January 5, 2015

Dear Daddy,

    Thank you for your letter. You made me laugh so much

when you talked about the dog picture you drew for me. You are right, it looked just like a hot dog with wheels. I also remember how hard we laughed. I do miss laughing like that with you. But I laugh a lot here, can you hear it? I especially laugh a lot with Mommy, she is so funny. I get visited a lot by the tickle monster!

Mommy is so beautiful. I do remember when you showed me the picture from your wedding. Mommy is just as beautiful now as she was when the picture was taken. She said to say hi to you. So, hi from Mommy. Mommy and me play a lot of board games together. We like to play Candyland and Chutes and Ladders. I win most of the time, Mommy says I am so good that it is not fair!

I also play a lot of games with other children. I am real friendly with Taylor, Jordyn, and Laura. We play lots of stuff together, but I think dress-up is my favorite. There are so so many bins of dress-up clothes, way more than we had at the house. My favorite is when we dress up like princesses,

Mommy tells me that I look just like a real princess. Me and

the other girls also like to braid each other's hair. But dress-up

is not all that we do. We also play kick ball, tennis, swimming,

and soccer a lot. I am pretty good at everything. There is also a

really neat zip line that we are allowed to use. At the end of

the zip line, you fall right into a ball pit! After we finish

playing, we always have ice cream. The nice people here let us

have a lot of ice cream, and they even told us we do not have

to eat salad if we don't want to. This makes me very happy.

I am very lucky that the weather is always nice here

and there are no thunder storms. I sleep with Mommy every

night anyway, and she always tells me I do not need an excuse

to snuggle up to her. I like when she reads me stories before

bed, she does this every night. She also sings to me before bed.

She says she loves doing all these things because she didn't get

a chance to do them when she was sick, I am happy that she

isn't sick anymore.

You didn't fail me at all. It was the other driver who failed us, there was nothing that you could have done. I know that you would have done anything in the world to save me. I want you to be happy, I don't want you to be sad anymore. Like Mommy said, being sad isn't going to bring me or her back to you. Mommy is very smart, so you should listen to her. She teaches me a lot of things, even more than my teachers at kindergarten! Mommy told me that we all get smarter when we get to this place, even though there is no school here. I miss school a little bit, especially my friends Hailey and Dylan. Mommy said they probably miss me too.

Mommy wanted to know if you have been getting on with your life. Do you still see your friends? Have you been going to work? She says that it is important that you do these things, especially getting out of the house. I'm not sure what it means, but she said she doesn't want you to close yourself off from everything. She said that was super important.

I told Mommy about the picture you tried to draw, she was laughing so hard when I told her it looked like a hot dog with wheels. She said you were never able to draw well and your pictures always came out funny. She said that me and her had all the creative talent in the family.

Ok Daddy, I'm going to go now. I drew you another picture of Mommy and me playing soccer, I hope you like it. Maybe you can draw me a picture and send it with one of your letters. I can't wait to get your next letter. I love and miss you SO much.

Your Princess,
Hannah

CHAPTER XIII

Kenneth's brother Barry and his wife Michele sat in their newly refurbished kitchen ironing out details for Alex's first birthday party. Barry jokingly referred to Michele as a "professional house wife," her preferring the term to "stay-at-home" mom. He knew how much work it was to do Michele's job, and was happy their two young children were being raised by her instead of a nanny.

They were holding Alex's first birthday party in their pristine backyard, with there being more than enough space to accommodate the seventy-five guests Michele planned to invite. The backyard was split into two halves – one side had a swing set and a large grassy area where the tents would go, the other side housed an in-ground swimming pool. The entire yard was surrounded by a white picket fence. With the two children, the only thing missing from the proverbial "American Dream" was the dog; Michele was allergic, thus they had to settle on fish.

They were currently having a heated discussion over whether or not to invite Kenneth to the party.

"He is my brother Michele, how could I not invite him?"

"A – because he is a drunk. B – because he has not been the same person since Hannah passed away. I think he has gone off the deep end."

"So your solution is to abandon him when he may need us the most and deprive him of the only family he has left?"

"Who knows how he will act out at the party."

"You are asking me to shun my only brother, who has been to hell and back these past few years, simply on speculation. That is wrong, I would never ask you to do that."

"I do not have a brother."

"Don't be a wise ass, you know what I mean. And besides, you know how much Stacey loves to see him."

"Stacey used to love to see him. He is a different man now, you yourself have acknowledged that."

"Do you know any man who has been through what he has been through that would be unchanged or unaffected?"

"You told me not to speculate."

"Michele, you are being unreasonable and extremely childish. You are not helping the situation at all. The bottom line is that he is my brother and I am not going to exclude him from family events because you have an unreasonable fear that his presence will taint the party somehow. I will not slight him like that."

"All of our friends are going to be there. Your boss from the gallery will be there. What if he loses it?"

"My God, we would probably have to move if you were embarrassed in front of your friends." Barry paused for a bit then continued. "I am sorry, I do not mean to be snarky, I am just upset by this conversation. I want him there. If a situation arises, I will handle it."

And that ended the conversation. Truth be told, Barry did in fact have concerns over Kenneth's presence at the party, but he did not want to voice those concerns to Michele. Kenneth had in fact changed a lot since Hannah's death. He rarely left his house, stopped going to work, and as far as Barry knew, had been drinking quite heavily and taking a lot of pills. If he came to the party, a big "if," Barry was uncertain how he would react being among a large group of people, many of which would be screaming children. This worried Barry; however, Kenneth had done so much for Barry in his lifetime, he felt downright awful at the thought of not inviting him.

Barry decided that rather than asking him over the

phone, he would go see Kenneth in person and ask him.

CHAPTER XIV

It was about 12:30 pm on an otherwise quiet Saturday day when Kenneth's doorbell rang. He had been sitting on his living room couch, still in his sleep clothes, shades drawn, glass of bourbon in front of him. He did not move at first, assuming whoever was there to disrupt his "peace" would take the hint and leave. However, the bell rang a second time a minute later and he could hear his older brother Barry on the other side of the door shouting at Kenneth to let him in.

Growing up, Kenneth had always had a good relationship with Barry. Sure, they fought and argued like all brothers do, but Barry always looked after his younger brother. They were only three years apart, so when Barry was a senior in high school, Kenneth was a freshman. This meant that Kenneth would not get picked on by anyone out of fear of reprisal by Barry, the school's top football star, and his teammates. This provided Kenneth the luxury of utilizing his smart and often sarcastic mouth at will, which would have otherwise caught him a beating or two.

Barry loved Kenneth very much. When Barry was struggling to become a successful artist, Kenneth and Frannie provided a lot of financial support to him, even allowing him to live with them for a while. Barry had been particularly fond of Frannie. Once Barry was out on his own and had his own family, the two families often got together for dinners, outside of the traditional Sunday night family gatherings. Barry's children, particularly Stacey, loved Kenneth, who was little more than a big kid himself. In return, Kenneth loved Barry's children like they were his own and enjoyed playing dress-up with Hannah and Stacey, who were both about the same age.

Since Hannah's passing, however, like all of Kenneth's relationships, his relationship with his brother had taken a bit of a hit. Kenneth stopped going to Barry's house for meals, rarely returned his calls, and certainly had no more princess tea parties with his niece. He tried once, it was just too painful for him. It reminded him too much of Hannah, and the activities that the three of them used to participate in. Through no fault of Barry and Michele, Kenneth had tried to distance himself as much as possible from them.

After letting Barry ring the bell a third time and shout some more, Kenneth begrudgingly got up from the couch to answer the door. Barely brining himself to say hello to Barry, which came out more as a grunt, he let Barry in the house and walked back to the couch.

"I would hate to see how you greet the UPS man," Barry quipped. "It is a little dark in here Kenneth, how about a little light?" As he said that, he walked over to the windows and opened the shades, enveloping the house in sunshine for the first time in months. Barry was a bit taken aback at how disheveled the house had become, Kenneth having always been a fastidious "neat-freak."

"Have you eaten yet today?" Barry continued.

"No."

"So it is safe to assume that the bourbon is your breakfast?"

"If you came over here to give me a hard time about things, I am not interested." Kenneth shot back.

"I am not here to give you a hard time little brother, quite the opposite." Kenneth hated when Barry called him little brother. Barry continued, "first off, I am here to feed you, you need to eat. You cannot survive on a steady diet of bourbon and pills. I brought you your favorite, chicken parmesan hero from Spagnoli's, even you cannot turn that down. Get up and come into the kitchen and eat lunch with me."

Kenneth picked up his glass and followed Barry into the kitchen. Putting the kitchen light on, Barry observed that the mess in the living room continued into the kitchen, with at least two weeks' worth of mail scattered on the kitchen table and a number of dirty dishes filling the sink.

They both sat at the table, where Barry scooped up all the mail into a neat pile, creating room to eat. Thankfully, the restaurant had included paper plates with the order, Barry was unsure that Kenneth had any clean plates left in the house. He put Kenneth's sandwich on a plate in front of him, along with a 20 ounce bottle of Diet Coke. Barry got the same exact lunch and set it out in front of himself.

"Try a little soda instead of bourbon with the sandwich, bourbon and chicken parmesan do not exactly go together." Barry suggested.

Against his will, Kenneth began eating his sandwich.

Although he would not admit it to Barry, the sandwich tasted good. It was also the first food Kenneth had put inside his body in two or three days. It felt good. Putting his emotions aside, his logical mind knew that he had to coat his stomach if he was going to continue to drink at the rate he had been doing. His emotional mind did not really care if he lived or died, so it was a constant battle between the two.

"There is something I want to talk to you about." Barry said as he also began eating his lunch.

"Here we go." Kenneth retorted.

"I am here to discuss something positive, do not be so quick to assume that everyone that comes here is going to lecture or judge you."

"That is all everyone does. I cannot sit with people for more than ten minutes before they start grilling me about the eating, the drinking, getting out of the house, and taking better care of myself."

"Well, it is a good thing I am not everyone else. You do have to put yourself in other people's shoes a little bit, Ken. Everyone is sitting by and watching you waste away. People want to help but have no idea what to do. This has been very difficult for your family and friends."

"Difficult for them? How do you think it has been for me?" Kenneth angrily responded.

"Nobody is trying to downplay what has happened to you, we all share your grief and simply wish we could do more for you. Do not forget, we all loved Frannie and Hannah dearly, they were my sister in-law and niece. I loved Hannah like she was my own child and you know that. We just want to help you, that is all."

"I do not need anyone's help. Kind words and chicken parmesan are not going to bring them back. At the end of the day, you still have your wife and two children to hug, to cuddle, to teach, to take solace in. You have no idea what it is like to have all that ripped away from you."

"You are right, I do not." Barry responded. "But that does not mean that I, or anyone in your family for that matter, do not know what it is like to be compassionate. If you would just let us, we want to be here for you. We want to take some of the pain off of your plate and put it on ours. Let us help you."

They sat and ate in silence for a little while. While Barry was happy to see Kenneth eating and drinking something other than bourbon, he was very dismayed at his general demeanor. He seemed to be crumbling right before his eyes, and he, like everyone else, was at a complete loss as to how to help.

"What is the story with work?"

"There is no story, they told me to take as much time as I needed. So I am."

"And they are still paying you your full salary?"

"Yep."

"How long do you think they will keep doing that for?"

"I have no idea."

"Do you plan on going back to work there ever?"

"I highly doubt it."

"So what do you plan on doing then?"

"I have not given it any thought. I figured I would cross that bridge when I came to it."

"I just hope, for your sake, that there is still a bridge for you to cross." Barry lamented. "Are you still seeing the psychologist?"

"Every week."

"How has it been going? Have you been finding it helpful?"

"It is hard to say, how do you define helpful? I talk to him. He asks me a ton of questions. He constantly asks me how I am feeling, what I miss most about Hannah, how I see myself coping with her being gone, and any number of other stupid questions about the situation."

"Why do you find that the questions are stupid? Do you not feel that he is trying to help you?"

"They are stupid questions because there are no answers. How do you think I feel about losing Hannah? I am devastated, I am lost, I am empty. I struggle every god damned day to think of ways in which I can survive the day without her. Very often I struggle to come up with a reason to survive, what is the point? I have nothing. I keep coming back to the thought that Mother Nature is a very cruel woman in an unfair, unjust world."

"Are you taking all of your medication? Do you find them helpful at all?"

"I have been taking my medication, I do not feel any better. So I guess I would say that they are not working."

"Is it possible that the medication may not be doing

what they are supposed to because all you have coating your stomach is alcohol? Does the doctor know about your drinking?"

This line of questioning was making Kenneth angry. "Nothing is working dammit because I do not want it to Barry. I do not want to get over Hannah, I do not want to move on, I do not want to let her go."

Taking a break before continuing, Kenneth took a swig of bourbon, again in lieu of the Diet Coke he had been sipping. Changing subjects, Kenneth asked, "didn't you say that there was a reason you came over here, something you wanted to talk to me about?"

"Michele and I are throwing a first birthday party for Alex in two weeks and we would like you to be there."

Kenneth cringed at this sentence. He hated leaving the house, he hated crowds of people, and even more so, he hated interacting with them. However, he immediately felt mixed emotions, as he really did love his niece and nephew. This was a very complex request for him to process. After ruminating on this sentence for a few minutes, he finally responded.

"Where is the party going to be held?"

"It will be at our house in the backyard. No public spaces for you to navigate." Barry said, sensing Kenneth's discomfort. "We are having it catered in, the kids will all be in the pool, Dad will be there. We rented one of those big, bouncy castles that the kids love. It will be very low key, Michele and Stacey would love to see you."

"How many people are you expecting, is it just family?"

Barry hesitated at first. "It is going to be family and friends, about seventy-five in total."

Kenneth reacted to this information exactly as Barry had expected he would. Kenneth let out somewhat of a laugh, got up from his chair, and scoffed: "seventy-five people? You call that low key?"

"That does not mean that you have to interact with seventy-five people, and a lot of that tally will be children. It would be perfectly fine for you to only interact with the family Ken."

"I do not know Barry, look at me, I am a mess. I have not left this house in four days. I find it hard to believe Michele would want me there."

"Do not worry about Michele, of course she wants you there. You are part of her family."

"Sorry, but it is hard to believe that the Stepford Wife would want her degenerate brother in-law at one of her soirees."

As much as Barry hated when Kenneth called Michele a Stepford Wife, he let it go. "Kenneth, what on God's green Earth makes you consider yourself a degenerate? Because you are recovering from two very difficult life losses? Because you are grieving? You are doing the best that you or anybody in your shoes could be expected to do. I think getting out and being among family in a jovial setting would be good for you. Worst case scenario, if you are uncomfortable, you leave. But I do think that this would be a good step for you."

"I will think about it, ok? I am not saying no, but I need to take some time to process all of this and decide if I am comfortable with it."

"I will accept that answer. It would mean a lot to the family if you showed up and tried your hand at life again."

"I said I will think about it, now drop it."

Barry got up, wrapped the other uneaten half of Kenneth's sandwich in tin foil and put it, along with the Diet Coke, in the refrigerator. He would not dare touch his bourbon. He then loaded all the dirty dishes in the sink into the dishwasher and ran it. Kenneth thanked him and walked him to the front door. "Be good Kenneth, I love you." Barry said this as he hugged his little brother. Kenneth uttered a "thank you" and closed the front door behind him.

CHAPTER XV

Kenneth headed to his appointment with Dr. Kaplan, the first time he actually had a topic he wanted to talk about. It had only been a few days since Barry was at his house, inviting him to Alex's first birthday. He had been giving it a lot of thought, he had very mixed emotions about his attending and he wanted to get Dr. Kaplan's opinion on the topic.

He arrived at Dr. Kaplan's office on time but was still forced to spend ten minutes in the outdated waiting room. He picked up a *Car and Driver* magazine that was six months old. He flipped through the pages, merely passing the time and not actually reading any of the articles. Finally, Dr. Kaplan's patient exited the office with the doctor right behind her, who invited Kenneth to come into the office and have a seat on the couch.

Kenneth took a seat on the couch and Dr. Kaplan sat in the leather chair across from him. "How have you been?" Dr. Kaplan began.

"Not good. I am still not sleeping, but I have trouble getting out of bed. I spend one to two hours in the shower, letting the hot water drown out the sound of my sobbing and trying to dull the pain. I cry all the time. My heart hurts."

"That is a lot of information you just presented me with. Why is it, in your opinion, that you have so much trouble sleeping?"

"Because every time I close my eyes I see Hannah's face. Or, if I do not see her face, I just replay that accident over and over again. I wonder what I could have done differently to have avoided it. Maybe if I had driven a little bit slower or a little bit faster, that car would not have hit us. Maybe if we had not been singing together, I would have heard the sounds of screeching tires if there was such a sound. If we had stopped for ice cream like Hannah wanted, she would still be here with me today. The scenarios are endless."

"Kenneth, we have talked about this. You absolutely cannot blame yourself for Hannah's death. You were doing everything right, everything you were supposed to. It was the other car, driven by a severely intoxicated man, who caused the accident and Hannah's death. That is a fact, one that was never disputed by anyone. You can replay the situation over and over in your head and come up with a thousand different scenarios, but the end result still would have been the same. What if there had been more traffic? What if you had stopped to use the rest room after the movie? What if you never went to the movies at all that night? The situations are endless, and you are never going to progress in your healing if you keep trying to come up with more. You must let that part go.

Pretend your guilt is inside a suitcase you carry around with

you. Just set it down, it is that simple. Tell me about the

showers, how often do you do that, meaning sitting in the

shower for hours on end?"

"Nearly every day. I turn the water temperature up

really high. I am usually in there for one to two hours. I cry. I

sit and I cry."

"Does that sound like healthy behavior to you?"

"I do not think of it in terms of healthy or unhealthy, I

look at it as therapeutic. Remedial."

"You want to know what I think? First off, I think you

use the shower as a form of self-punishment. This is

particularly apparent in the fact that you turn the temperature

way up. Is it hot enough that is actually burns?"

"At first it does. But after a while, the pain dulls. Either

my body just accepts the pain or the nerve endings just dull.

Either way, it does not matter."

"I think your burning yourself is just an extension of the guilt you feel." Dr. Kaplan hypothesized. "You feel so guilty over Hannah's death that you are trying to punish yourself. But as we discussed before, you cannot blame yourself for Hannah's death. You need to let go of that guilt.

Secondly, I think you are using the time in the shower as a means of avoidance. I think you are using it as a means of avoiding life, of avoiding your pain, of avoiding your reality. The longer you spend in the shower, the less time you have to spend in the outside world. The same goes for spending hours in bed."

"I do not disagree with that." Kenneth retorted in a somewhat patronizing tone that was intended to placate Dr. Kaplan. Kenneth was sick and certainly depressed, but he was not stupid. He could still put on his "attorney hat" when needed and manipulate conversations as he deemed necessary. Kenneth was not trying to be patronizing, he just wanted to shift the focus of the conversation to what he wanted to talk about.

"My brother Barry came to see me the other day." he began. "He wanted to know if I would attend my nephew's first birthday party. It is being held at his house, it is a pool party. They are expecting about seventy-five people. I am on the fence about whether or not to go. I wanted your opinion on this."

"Well, let's talk this out. First off, you have barely left the house in weeks except for our appointments. How would you feel going to a party with seventy-five people?"

"Barry said that I would only have to interact with my family members."

"That may be so, but you will still be surrounded by a very large group of people. You have expressed to me that you have difficulty being around people in stores or on the street, and that is just a fraction of the number of people you are talking about."

"I understand. But it is outdoors, their backyard is very large and spacious, so I feel that people would not be right on top of me. I feel somewhat obligated, I love my niece and nephew. I would not want to let them down."

"Let me ask you, would Alex know or remember if you were at his first birthday party?"

"That is not the point, I would know."

"Ok, let us put aside the crowd for a second. Let us talk about what I think is my real concern. This party will be filled with young children, no? You have also expressed to me how seeing children exacerbates your depression as they make you think of Hannah. Am I correct?"

"That is true, and something I have been thinking about. And it is something that I imagine might be tough. But I have got to start somewhere, sometime, don't I? Those were your words."

"Yes, but you are leaving out some of my qualifying language. Primarily, baby steps. I am not adverse to you starting to get out of the house, increasing your human interaction, maybe attend a support group or two. But a large party filled with children is not a baby step. That is jumping right into the deep end. I recommended that you leave the house and go to a store, a mall, some place outside your home that might not be filled with triggers to start. Build yourself up to something like a party. I just do not want to see you crash and burn on your first outing; that could set our progress back quite a bit."

"So you are recommending that I do not go?"

"I do not think it would be the wisest idea from a psychological standpoint. However, should you decide to attend, I highly recommend that you have a safety plan in place in case you get overwhelmed. You know that you can call me anytime and as long as I am not with a patient, I will talk to you. You should also talk to Barry ahead of time and advise him that he should not be alarmed if you do get overwhelmed and have to excuse yourself indoors or leave the party altogether. I would also advise him that you do not need to be introduced to all seventy-five people. Stick to your family, stay within the limits of your comfort zone. Plan ahead.

I reiterate, however, that I do not think it is a great idea for you to go. And you know I only have your best interests and health in mind. I am less concerned with Barry's feelings than I am with your health."

"Thank you for the honesty, I will certainly weigh everything you had to say today. If I go, maybe it will be a big step towards my recovery, or maybe it will be a colossal failure. I will not know if I do not try."

And with that, their session ended. Kenneth walked

out feeling good about the session. Dr. Kaplan, however, was less pleased, feeling very nervous for Kenneth. The most he could do, however, was give his best advice, which he felt he did, and hope for the best.

CHAPTER XVI

The night before Alex's birthday, Kenneth did not sleep well. Not that this was a surprise to him, as he never slept well, but this had been a particularly bad night. When he was not fading in and out of nightmares, he was up taking pill after pill trying to knock himself out. Thorazine. Trazadone. Xanax. Klonopin. He took so much medication that he eventually just found himself in somewhat of a twilight, a daze during which images of Hannah floated by him. He would reach out to try and catch them, but they always remained just outside his grasp.

The stage for disaster was set during these events. The party was called for 2:30 pm, which gave Kenneth plenty of time to try and clean himself up and get himself prepared for what lie ahead of him. At some level, he knew he was going to fail; what remained uncertain was how that failure would manifest itself and what its magnitude would be. He began drinking around 9:00 am, on top of the nighttime medications he took in.

To Kenneth's credit, he shaved for the first time in weeks and got "dressed up," which for him, consisted of a pair of Khaki shorts and a Polo shirt. He was a bit taken aback at how loose the shorts were, he apparently had lost more weight than he had realized. After he shaved, he stared at his face in the mirror for a long time. He looked gaunt, his eyes hallowed and bloodshot, his cheek bones protruding. This image frightened him; he actually could not remember the last time he had looked upon himself. He looked lifeless. Before long, he realized he was crying. Klonopin, dose number three since 3:00 am.

The afternoon rolled around quickly, quicker than he would have liked. He was feeling very anxious. He put in a call to Dr. Kaplan, but got his voicemail. He left the doctor a message, asking for a return phone call if possible. He left his cell phone number, which was ironic because Kenneth could not remember having seen or looked at his cell phone in weeks. Kenneth knew that Dr. Kaplan was against his going to the party; however, he felt he could at least benefit from a few words of encouragement. He was not sure of anyone else he could call on that front, not wanting to bother his best friend Ricky.

As he prepared to leave the house, it dawned on him that he did not get Alex a birthday present. He grabbed his checkbook, wrote a check to Alex for $500, and put it in a white envelope. He wrote Alex's name on the front of the envelope. This makeshift card and gift would have to do. He took one more Xanax and filled his flask with bourbon, and secured both items in his short's pockets. The flask, ironically, had once been a gift from his brother Barry. He got in his car and made the fifteen minute drive over to Barry's house.

Kenneth arrived at the house approximately fifteen minutes after the party started, finding it surprisingly difficult to find a place to park. Barry had apparently not exaggerated about the seventy-five person guest list. Kenneth found a place up the block to park. Walking up to Barry's house, he could see the inflatable castle soaring high above the fence surrounding the property. He could also hear the sound of children laughing and screaming, sounds which stopped him dead in his tracks in Barry's front yard. He felt short of breath, and briefly considered turning around and going home. Somehow he worked up the courage to continue onwards.

He walked through the gate on the side of the house that did not contain the pool, and immediately spotted his father and his niece sitting at a table together. He approached the table, as soon as Stacey saw him she ran into his arms.

"Uncle Kenny, I didn't know you were coming. You look so different!"

"Hi sweetheart," Kenneth said as he lifted her up, "I would not miss an opportunity to see my favorite girl."

"Come and watch me in the bouncy house, c'mon c'mon."

"In a little bit, I promise, let me talk to Grandpa first. Also, where are Mommy and Daddy."

"They are over by the pool."

"Ok sweetie, go play and I promise I will come watch you soon. give me a big kiss first." Stacey obliged and planted a big kiss right on Kenneth's sunken cheek.

Kenneth walked over to his father, greeted him, and told him he would be right back after he said hello to Barry and Michele. He walked over to the "pool side" and approached his brother and sister in-law, all the while feeling the eyes of all the guests burning a hole in his back. Pity was not his friend. Barry and Michele greeted him, rather coolly he felt, Michele seeming hesitant to hand Alex over to him.

"We are glad you were able to make it, and all shaved and dressed up too, it's nice to see." Michele said, a hint of sarcasm in her voice. She reluctantly handed Alex over to him, asking him if he was ok to hold him.

"Thanks for having me," Kenneth replied. Kenneth noticed his hands faintly shaking as he held Alex, but he tried to ignore this. He handed the folded up envelope with the check to Michele, who quipped that "Hallmark is getting less creative every year, huh?" Kenneth did not laugh at this, neither did Barry.

Barry sensed Kenneth's discomfort and immediately took Alex back from him and handed him to Michele. "Excuse us for a moment sweetie," Barry said as he grabbed Kenneth by the arm and pulled him off to the side.

"What are you on?" Barry asked him pointedly.

"What are you talking about?"

"You look stoned, completely stoned. Your eyes are as glassy and red as marbles, you are slurring your words, you reek of bourbon, and do not think for one second that I did not see your hands shaking while you were holding Alex. What the hell is the matter with you?"

"You are the one who pressured me into coming here."

"I wanted my son's uncle to show up, clear-eyed and clear-headed. I was not expecting Hunter Thompson to show up."

"So it is my fault that your expectations were entirely unrealistic?"

"Kenneth, go get yourself a bottle of water and sit with Dad. Get yourself together or go home." Barry then walked away from him and rejoined his wife.

Kenneth walked towards the table set up with an

assortment of beverages in coolers, including water, beer, and

hard liquor. There were also several bottles of soda on the

table. Ensuring that nobody was watching him, he took the

flask from his pocket and filled a red Solo cup half full of

bourbon. He then poured a bit of soda into the cup just in case

anyone was watching, he would keep up the image of sobriety

for as long as possible, at least for Barry's sake.

He took his cup to where his father was sitting and sat

down next to him. At first, neither of them spoke. His father

just looked at him with a sense of bewilderment, neither of

them knowing what to say. Finally, his father spoke:

"Kenneth, you look terrible. When was the last time you slept

or ate?"

"It has been a while. I do not know, how many days has

it been since I buried my heart and soul in the ground?"

"You do not have to be sarcastic with me, I am just

concerned about you. I have not seen you in almost a month

and you never return my phone calls. Do you ever go outside, you look as pale as a sheet?"

"No, I do not make it outside very often, there is little point. I have nowhere to go."

"It would not kill you to come visit your father once in a while. Are you keeping up with your psychology appointments?"

"Yes, I go once a week. I am also keeping up with my medications. Is there anything else you want to ask?" Kenneth was not normally this short with his father.

"Again, Kenneth, there is no need to be nasty, I am only trying to help you if you'll let me. You clearly are not eating, you look like a concentration camp victim."

"Comments, questions, and grilling like this are the exact reasons I do not come over or return phone calls. It is not helpful, I would actually say it is counter-productive. Kenneth's voice started to rise during his response with a few people at the nearest table turning towards them. Kenneth's father raised his arms in an effort to calm him down, and said: "Kenneth, please relax, this is a celebration, not a place to be raising your voice. What I am trying to tell you is that I am worried about you. At the same time, I am hurting with you. You have always let me help you in the past, let me help you now."

As soon as his father stopped talking, Kenneth did not respond, instead choosing to get up from the table and walk away. He was in no kind of mood to be lectured, it seemed that is all everyone did to him. Everyone had suggestions and advice. What these same people were missing were the traumas that Kenneth had endured.

He took his cup, which was nearly empty at this point, and walked over to the bouncy castle. He saw Stacey in the castle jumping and screaming, "Uncle Kenny, watch me do a flip." She did two back flips and Kenneth clapped for her.

Before she could do another flip, a boy who was a lot larger than her ran into her and knocked her down, causing her to start crying. Kenneth immediately went into the bouncy castle to get her and comfort her. As he reached her, he also came upon the young boy who had knocked into her. Surprising even himself, he grabbed the boy by the shirt and yelled: "why don't you watch where you are going, you could hurt somebody playing that way. What the hell is the matter with you?" The boy immediately started crying. Unbeknownst to Kenneth, the boy's father was standing right there watching the scene unfold.

The boy's father climbed into the bouncy castle and yelled at Kenneth to get his hands off of his son. Kenneth responded in kind by yelling back that the boy was being too aggressive and knocked Stacey over. At this point, every person at the party had stopped what they were doing to watch what was going on between Kenneth and the man.

Barry quickly hurried over to diffuse the situation, not wanting any further escalation. Once he saw that Stacey was ok, he grabbed Kenneth by the arm and pulled him towards the house.

"Ok everyone, let's get back to the party," Barry said. "The food will be here shortly so everyone enjoy themselves."

Barry half-dragged Kenneth inside the house, not saying anything to him until they were upstairs in Barry's bedroom.

"What the fuck is wrong with you?" Barry yelled at his baby brother.

"There is nothing wrong with me." Kenneth replied with an obvious slur in his words. "That kid knocked Stacey over and made her cry."

"Do you know who "that kid" was? That was the gallery owner's son. And that was the gallery owner, my boss, that you were yelling at."

"I do not care who it was, I am always going to protect my family."

"Kenneth, it is a bouncy house. Kids always bump into each other and get bumps and bruises. Have you never been to a kid's birthday-" Barry stopped himself before he finished this sentence, immediately realizing what a delicate subject he was about to touch on. But it was too late. Kenneth sat down on Barry's bed and began to sob. In between sobs, he was able to get out that he misses Hannah so much. Barry sat down on the bed next to Kenneth and put his arm around him. Kenneth in turn hugged Barry tightly, burying his face in Barry's shoulder. This caught Barry a little off guard, showing emotion in front of his older brother was not something Kenneth usually did. Barry hugged him back.

"I know you do Ken, we all do. Stacey asks about her all the time, and Michele and I loved her like she was our own. We all know how much you are hurting, but you do not let any of us help you."

Kenneth continued to cry for a few minutes in Barry's arms. "I need to go home," Kenneth finally uttered. Barry admonished him, "you cannot possibly think that I am letting you get behind the wheel of a car in your current condition."

"I'm fine." Kenneth replied. "I just need some water."

"Ken, you of all people should appreciate the dangers of driving drunk, I do not need to and will not explain myself further."

At this point, Michele walked into the bedroom, visibly annoyed. "Are you planning on rejoining your son's birthday party?"

"I am going to drive Kenneth home," Barry replied.

"No you most certainly are not. I told you this was a horrible idea from the start. The food is going to be here any minute, I am not setting it up and entertaining seventy-five people by myself. Either you have your father drive him home and he can pick up his car tomorrow, or else just let him pass out here. I do not want him outside again while our guests are here, he is drunk and lord knows what else."

"Take it easy Michele, he is going through a rough time."

"Do not tell me to take it easy Barry. He was not able to make it thirty minutes without causing a scene. He should not have been here in the first place."

"MICHELE," Barry shouted, "he is my brother and he is sitting right here. Stop saying such hurtful things, now."

"Oh please, you think he is going to remember a single word I say? Look at him, he can barely even hold himself upright."

"Fine. I will have Dad drive him home. Happy?"

"Thrilled." Michele said sarcastically as she stormed out of the bedroom.

"Kenneth," Barry said, returning his attention to his

little brother, "Dad is going to drive you home and I will bring your car back to you tomorrow. Go home and try to get some rest. I love you, do not pay attention to Michele, parties just make her a bit high strung. I will call you tomorrow."

Barry and his father helped load Kenneth into the car. Kenneth's father and him made the fifteen minute drive back to Kenneth's house in silence. When they arrived at the house, Kenneth's father helped him inside and into his bedroom. Kenneth kicked off his shoes and passed out immediately face down on his bed. His father stared at him for a brief minute, a tremendous sense of sadness came over him as he observed what had become of his son. He went and got a bottle of water, which he left on the bed side table. He then leaned down, kissed Kenneth on the head, and whispered: "I love you son." He let himself out and slowly drove back to the party.

Kenneth's horrible day had finally come to an end.

CHAPTER XVII

Two days following Alex's birthday party Kenneth had an appointment with Dr. Kaplan. Arriving on time, Kenneth sheepishly entered Dr. Kaplan's office, not doubting for one second that he was in for a professional case of "I told you so."

"So," Dr. Kaplan began, "how did the party go?"

"Exactly as you predicted, I should have listened to you. I want to get that out of the way right from the get-go. It was an incredible disaster."

"Tell me about it."

"The night before, I did not sleep. I took a shit-ton of medication, all different kinds of pills, in an effort to get myself to sleep. All that accomplished was to get me so stoned I could barely see straight. I began drinking at around 9:00 am. By the time the party rolled around, I was in no condition to be going anywhere, let alone a children's party."

"Why do you think you had so much trouble sleeping the night before?"

"I was so nervous and anxious about the party, I could not get it out of my mind. And then I started thinking about all the children that were going to be there, and how much fun Hannah would have had being there."

"Let me ask you, if you felt so miserable, why did you not just call Barry in the morning and tell him that you were not going to be able to make it?"

"After all the pills, I was not thinking clearly. I had convinced myself that I was able to go. I shaved, got myself dressed. I thought I could do it."

"Ok, so what happened next?"

"I had a little more to drink at the party. I was not there for a thirty minutes before I caused a scene." Kenneth recapped the bouncy castle incident to Dr. Kaplan, or at least what he remembered of it, which involved his yelling at a child. His brother's boss's child nonetheless. He vaguely recalled the conversation with Barry in his bedroom, and he clearly remembered Michele yelling at Barry, saying that Kenneth should not have been there in the first place. Everything thereafter was hazy.

"Are you willing to accept now that you have a drinking problem?"

"No, I characterize someone with a drinking problem when they want to stop but cannot. I do not want to stop drinking. Despite these past events, it still serves an important purpose in dulling my pain and making the days more tolerable."

"Kenneth, you almost ruined your nephew's first

birthday party and potentially could have gotten your brother in trouble with his boss. Does this not mean anything to you?"

"Of course they mean something to me, but you were right in that I should not have been in that situation in the first place. The children laughing and screaming was what put me over the edge, not the alcohol. All I could think about was Hannah, and how she belonged at that party."

"Well, I wish I could say that I did not warn you. You need to take baby steps to re-integrate back into society. But I do not want you to completely beat yourself up over this situation, let us try and find some positives. You got out of the house, you cleaned yourself up, you went to a large gathering. These are all positive steps that you can use in your recovery, just on a smaller scale. Perhaps now you will be more amenable to my suggestions that you get out into less crowded environments, such as stores or parks. Also, perhaps you will take my suggestion and look into loss support groups? These types of situations should be a bit more in your grasp now that you see you can do it."

"But that is not entirely accurate. I was not able to do it, even with all the drugs and alcohol. I failed."

"You did not fail, you tried and it did not work out. It may be hard to believe or hard to hear, but I am proud of you. This is tremendous progress, and I do not want you to beat yourself up over it. Ok?"

"I do not see how that is possible, but ok. I will try. By the way, I did try and call you before the party for some words of encouragement, but I got your voicemail. I left you a message asking you to call me back, but you never did."

"I know and I apologize. I was away for the weekend and we had no cell phone service where we were. I assure you that will not happen again, I want you to feel that you can count on me."

They ended the session on that note, with Dr. Kaplan

reiterating that Kenneth should be proud of himself and not

beat himself up over the party. Kenneth had a hard time

swallowing this, but what was done was done.

CHAPTER XVIII

Kenneth read Hannah's latest letter and gave a lot of thought to the questions Hannah had proposed to him. He found the answers were almost uniformly "no." He rarely left the house save for an occasional trip to the grocery store or the liquor store. And of course, his trips to the mailbox to mail his letters to Hannah. He had not been back to work, and had lost contact with just about all of his friends, which was his own fault. They all repeatedly reached out to him following the accident, but he never felt up to visitors. He did not like feeling pitied. Eventually, one by one, they stopped calling. It had not really dawned on him until now, but he truly lived a solitary existence. And he was fine with that; he thought so at least.

He was not sure what prompted him to call Ricky, his best friend for more than twenty years. Ricky tried his best to be there for Kenneth after Hannah's passing, but Kenneth rejected his help just as he did with all the others. Kenneth and Ricky had gone to grade school and college together. After college, Ricky went to work in the insurance industry while Kenneth went to law school. Kenneth was not one of those people who pined to be a lawyer since they were in the womb; he just was not ready to be an adult and he realized he could fuel his Peter Pan Syndrome with three more years of schooling.

Kenneth had not spoken to him in months, so he was a bit shocked at Ricky's reaction to the phone call. Kenneth asked him if he could come over to talk, and Ricky jumped at the opportunity because he genuinely wanted his best friend back. It was a weekend so Ricky was able to come right over.

Kenneth greeted Ricky at the door, still in his sleep clothes, and several days unshaven. Ricky immediately noticed that Kenneth reeked of alcohol, and it was only 1:00 pm. Kenneth offered Ricky a drink as they sat on opposing sofas in the living room, which Ricky politely turned down. Ricky asked if they could turn the lights on or even better, open the shades to get some sunlight in the house. Kenneth obliged.

As soon as the sunlight hit Kenneth, Ricky could not suppress his gasp. Kenneth looked like he had aged ten years over the past few months. His eyes were sunken, his skin was leathery, and he was clearly emaciated. Ricky assumed this was the result of feverishly drinking in constant darkness. This was not the vibrant, good-looking lawyer he had been best friends with for so long. What sat before him was a shell of a human being. Kenneth's appearance brought on a strong feeling of sadness in Ricky, and he had to fight back tears.

"When was the last time you ate?" Ricky asked.

"Not sure, why?"

"Do you want to go out and get some food?"

"No."

"Can I go get you some food?"

"No."

"What time did you start drinking today?"

"What's the difference?"

"Why did you call me over?"

"I wanted to talk to you and tell you the most amazing thing that has happened."

"I'm all ears old friend."

"I have been receiving letters from Hannah."

This caught Ricky completely off guard, and he had to collect his thoughts before responding. He had feared the worst coming over to Kenneth's house, and his fears, although not the ones he predicted, were being confirmed. Kenneth had completely lost his mind.

"What are you talking about?" Ricky sadly inquired.

"My psychologist recommended that I write to Hannah as sort of a healing exercise. A way to vent my feelings. I took it one step further and actually mailed my letter to Hannah in Heaven. And you wouldn't believe it, but she actually wrote me back! Several times already."

"What has your psychologist said about this?"

"He was very negative about the situation, he says that it is impossible and someone is essentially playing a joke on me. But he does not know what he is talking about."

"Do you hear yourself Kenneth? Do you have any idea how crazy you sound?"

"What is so crazy about it? She answers my letters, answers questions I ask her, all with the help of Frannie. Frannie found Hannah and they are together all the time. Frannie helps Hannah read my letters and helps her write responses."

"Look, Kenneth, I've been your best friend for more than twenty years. When you cut me off after you lost Hannah, I felt hurt and wronged. At least I deserved the respect of a hug goodbye. But I got over it, that is why I am here today. Now I loved Frannie and Hannah like they were my own family, you know that. There are not many people who wish every day that they were still with us other than me. But they are gone Kenneth. What you are describing to me is pure lunacy. You have spent a countless number of days and nights holed up in this house, in complete darkness, and apparently drinking a shit-ton of bourbon. Your judgment and your perception of reality are clouded to say the least."

"I am very worried about you," Ricky continued. "We all are. My family, our friends, your own family. You have cut yourself off from everyone. People want to help you, but you will not let anyone in."

"I DON'T WANT ANYONE'S HELP DAMMIT,"

Kenneth yelled while slamming his glass of bourbon down on

the table. "I did not ask for anyone's help, I am getting by just

fine. I am rejuvenated by these letters from Hannah."

"Hannah is dead Kenneth," Ricky shouted right back at

him.

"Do you think I don't know that? But there is a higher

power at work here. These letters are genuine, she writes

about things that only she and I would know."

"She writes about stuff only she and you would know,

or does she just respond to things you write in letters to her?"

"Why can't you let me have this? You are supposed to

be my best friend, why are you shitting all over the best thing

that has happened to me since the accident. Not only the best

thing, the only good thing. You won't even let me have this

happiness.

That's enough, get the fuck out of my house and out of

my life. I don't need or want you and your negativity in my life. I'm sorry I called you over."

"Kenneth, you are drunk, don't do this. Do not say things you will regret when you sober up, whenever that may be."

"The only thing I regret is you coming over here today. Get out."

And with that, Ricky got up and headed to the front door. He took one last moment to look at Kenneth. With tears in his eyes, Ricky implored Kenneth to listen to reason and talk this out with him. Kenneth refused and again told Ricky to get out. And he did.

CHAPTER XIX

Kenneth felt enraged by his visit with Ricky and decided to take a long, hot shower to try and relax. Who the hell was Ricky to try and tell him how he should be coping with his losses? He had no idea what he had been going through, nobody did. This was his cross to bear. His and his alone. There was not anything anyone could say that was going to bring Frannie and Hannah back, so the letters from Hannah were that much more meaningful and important to him.

When he got out of the shower, he noticed the clock and that it was later than he realized. He skipped dinner in lieu of another glass of bourbon and some Klonopin. He was not much of a cook to begin with, Frannie had been the real chef of the family. She was always reading *Good Housekeeping* for new recipes to try. While some panned out better than others, Kenneth was always excited to try her latest concoctions, good or bad. Kenneth always told Frannie that the meals tasted like they were made with love.

After Frannie passed, Kenneth set out to be the best father a person could be, for he wanted to keep his promise to Frannie that he would devote his life to raising Hannah. He temporarily left his job, the partners at the law firm agreeing to allow him to go out on an indefinite, paid leave. He did not have to worry about money; they had saved quite a bit over the years and Frannie also had a significant life insurance policy in place. Kenneth had never been so upset depositing a check before. He remained out of work for nearly a year. When he returned to work, his father would assist with the day-to-day duties of watching Hannah.

As Hannah grew up, her bond with Kenneth grew stronger by the day. She started walking, talking, and generally became a well-adjusted young girl. Kenneth cherished his time and moments with Hannah, such as teaching her to ride a bike, having princess tea parties, watching Disney movies, and doing art projects together. Hannah was his whole world and vice versa. As soon as she was old enough, Kenneth made sure to talk to her about Frannie and show her pictures and videos of her. She learned to identify her, referring to her as "mama."

It was a very difficult day when Kenneth had to explain where "mama" was. Hannah came home from her pre-kindergarten class asking why she did not have a mommy like the other children. Apparently, one of the student's mothers came into Hannah's class to read to the students. Hannah was four years old at the time. Kenneth sat her down and explained that when Hannah was just a baby, Mommy got very sick. Hannah asked if it was a cold like she sometimes gets, to which Kenneth replied "sort of." He explained that Mommy was so sick that she could not live in this world anymore, and that she was now in Heaven looking down upon them.

"Will I ever get to see her again?" Hannah asked as she began to cry.

"You will probably see her when you go to Heaven, but that will not be for many, many years from now. You have your whole life ahead of you."

"It's not fair, why isn't Mommy here?"

Kenneth again explained that Mommy got very sick and could not get better. He could not think of how else to explain it, and he hoped he was doing the right thing.

"But how come all the other children have a mommy?"

"Sometimes life just isn't fair Princess and bad things happen to good people. But you have me, and I will never leave you."

"Is Mommy still sick?"

"No Princess, where Mommy is, nobody is sick."

"Can she see us?"

"I think that she is looking down at us at all times. And there are times that I feel she is right here in the room with us."

"Will I ever feel that way?"

"You probably will."

"Did Mommy ever play with me when I was little?"

Kenneth began to tear up, despite his desire to not let Hannah see him crying. "You bet she did Princess. She did her best to spend as much time as possible with you, even when she started to get sick. She loved to cuddle with you, you were the "apple of her eye." That means she loved you and cherished being with you. Mommy had one of the nicest laughs, when she laughed, it made everyone around her laugh. And you were no different. When she laughed, you would giggle alongside her."

"I feel sad that she isn't here." Hannah said through her tears.

Kenneth hugged her tight as she sobbed into his sweat shirt and Kenneth began to cry as well. "I know you wish she was here Princess. I think about Mommy every day and wish she was still here. It hurts me to think about all that she is missing, it hurts me to see you growing up without Mommy getting to see all the milestones you are reaching. It also hurts me because Mommy was my best friend for many years, not just my wife. It is ok to feel sad. I do not want you to think it is wrong to feel sad, it is perfectly normal. I cry a lot too when I think about Mommy. But when I feel sad, I try to think about all he happy memories and moments I shared with her. I think about how beautiful she was, I think about her laugh and her smile, I think of vacations we took together. And when I think about those things, it makes me feel happy."

"But I don't remember anything like that, I don't have my own memories of Mommy, I don't remember good times I had with her."

Kenneth paused after hearing this comment. Hannah was only four years old, but this was a statement that showed a cognitive development well beyond her years, and a sentiment to which he did not know exactly how to respond.

"Even though you may not remember good times you had with her, I can tell you that you did have the chance to laugh with Mommy, and you two had fun together. She loved to read books to you, in fact, she read a different story to you every night before we put you to bed."

"Just like you do now?"

"That's right. Mommy was a school teacher, and she felt it was very important that we never miss an opportunity to read to you. That is probably why you are so smart."

After a long pause, Hannah continued: "I wish Mommy was still here."

"I do too Princess, I do too," Kenneth concluded.

After that, the two of them sat there in silence for a long while, Kenneth hugging her tightly. Together, they cried.

CHAPTER XX

After reminiscing to himself about Frannie and

Hannah, Kenneth set out to write his latest letter to Hannah.

He was a wound-up ball of emotions following his visit with

Ricky and thoughts of Frannie's illness. He was not sure if this

was the right state of mind to write her, but he figured that

uncertainty was nothing that a glass of bourbon and a

Klonopin couldn't help.

March 6, 2015

Dear Princess Hannah,

I am so happy to hear that you made some nice friends

where you are, I was worried that you would be all alone. It sounds like you are having a lot of fun. I am very jealous of all the time you get to spend with Mommy, I miss her a lot too. Just like I miss you, but it sounds like the tickle monster found you. I am happy there are dress-up clothes, do you have princess tea parties like we used to have? You used to dress me up in the funniest outfits. My favorite was the king's outfit, but we would laugh the most when you dressed me up as a princess. I still laugh thinking about that.

In response to Mommy's questions, the answers are generally no. I went back to work about one year after she left me, but have not been back to work since you left me. I have not really talked to or seen our friends either, the pain of losing you has just been too overbearing.

Every day is a struggle for me, as I am always trying to make sense of what happened to you. Not a moment goes by when I am not thinking about you. You can tell Mommy that I am working with a nice doctor to help me get better. But it is just so hard without you here, I miss my best friend, my partner in crime.

I went into the IHOP the other day, the one we used to go to where you would order the "funny-face" pancake. You loved that place. I sat at our usual table and had Cheryl, our usual waitress, serve me. She began to cry when I told her what happened to you, as she had asked why she had not seen us in a while. She said that you were one of the most beautiful and well-behaved children she had ever served. I ordered my usual eggs and hash browns, and I ordered a "funny-face" pancake with no strawberries for you out of habit. That was a very difficult experience for me.

To be honest with you Princess, Daddy is not in a very happy place. Without you here, I do not have anyone to have fun with. Someday, I will join you and Mommy where you are, and we will be a complete family again. We will do all the things we used to do together. And Mommy will be part of it too. I long for that day.

I saw your "uncle" Ricky the other day, but I was not very nice to him. I feel bad about it now because he was just trying to help me. In response, I asked him to leave the house and not come back. I feel bad having done that, it is just very hard for me to relate to people anymore. Nobody else is going through what I am going through, and nobody can identify with the pain of having lost both you and Mommy. Nobody understands how hard it is to go to sleep and wake up every day in a quiet house. I would not wish this on anyone.

I am sorry that this has been such a sad letter. Let's talk about fun things. I cannot believe how much ice cream you have been eating! You used to love mint pistachio ice cream, is that what you have or do you try others? Mommy's favorite ice cream was vanilla chip, is that what she has? I think it is great that you get to play so often, especially kick ball and tennis. I love playing kick ball; maybe someday I'll get to play with you, which would be so much fun.

Tell me about your friends Taylor, Jordyn, and Laura. Are they the same ages as you? What types of things do you like to do together? Do you do any arts and crafts together? That was always one of your favorite activities. Do you remember the time we made a bird house together out of popsicle sticks and glue? We then painted it pink and purple, your favorite colors. Guess what? It is still hanging from the tree and there is a family of birds living in it! Every morning I sit out on the deck and watch the little birdies go in and out of it.

The zip line sounds like a lot of fun, especially because you land in a ball pit. You always loved doing the zip line at birthday parties! Do you like the ball pit? I know I would never let you go in them when you were here because they were too dirty. I am sure that is not the case there, so I am glad you are able to use them.

Do you get to swim? You worked so hard during your swim lessons this past summer. You were my little fishy, remember I used to call you Nemo? Nicole was such a good teacher, the two of you laughed and splashed around every lesson. I hope that you have had a chance to show Mommy how good you swim, and that you can even put your face under water!

Ok Princess, I am going to bed now. I love and miss you THIS much.

Love,
Daddy

CHAPTER XXI

Kenneth sat across from Dr. Kaplan, hands on his knees, knees shaking back and forth. Dr. Kaplan was wearing his usual shirt and tie, sleeves rolled up to his elbows.

"Our last session ended well, one of our better sessions I would say." Dr. Kaplan began. "Are you ready to discuss your correspondence with Hannah?"

"I do not want to talk about my letters to Hannah."

"Fine by me, it is your dime. But you do realize that we are going to have to address that topic at some point. If I may be perfectly frank, I think you are suffering from paranoid delusions, among other things."

"I feel empty. I try to find meaning in my everyday life,

but I am constantly coming up short. I am not motivated to do anything. I am not motivated to talk to anyone. I spend my days in the house, shades drawn, phone off the hook. Bourbon is my only friend, and I spend a lot of time with her."

"Have you given any thought to going back to work in any capacity?"

"No, there is no way I would be able to concentrate or focus on any work. I have enough trouble reading the comics in the newspaper."

"Ok, let us start smaller. Have you given any thought to getting out of the house more often?"

"No, I do not see the purpose. There is nothing out there for me."

"There could be numerous benefits. The sun will feel good on your skin, get a little vitamin D on your body. Go to stores or the park, places where you could start having interactions with people. Make an effort to reconnect with the human race."

"Are you being sarcastic?"

"Not at all. I am simply trying to offer you suggestions of ways to slowly come out of your shell and integrate back into society."

"You are making a big presumption that I want to integrate back into society. To me, that is a society that turned its back on me. First, it took Frannie from me, well before it should have been her time to go. Somehow, I managed to pick up the pieces of my life and "reintegrate" into society, knowing that I had a daughter to raise. And I devoted my life to that task and did a damned good job. I loved her more than one would think possible. I gave her everything I had to offer and more. And what happened? She was ripped away from me, she was a victim of a brutal society. She was only five years old. Where is the justice in that? How could you expect me to want to insert myself back into that society?"

"Because you are still here, you have a life to live. Frannie and Hannah would want that, they would both want you to get out of the house and be a person again."

"How do you know that? Hannah did not say anything like that in her letter to me."

This last statement made Dr. Kaplan pause as he knew he was again treading on fragile territory.

"What did Hannah say to you in her letters?" Dr. Kaplan inquired.

"I told you, I do not want to talk about it."

"Ok, so I ask again, what do you want to talk about?"

"I don't know. I just feel empty. I try to put the television on to distract me but I just find it to be an annoyance. I had an interaction with Ricky for the first time in months."

"That's a great development. Did you reach out to him or vice versa?"

"It was not a great development, it was actually a horrible experience. I called him and asked him to come over."

"Regardless of the outcome, the fact that you reached out to him in and of itself is a positive development. That is a big step."

"I called him over because I wanted to tell him about the letters I have been receiving from Hannah. Something that I was actually excited about, and something that, as my best friend, he should have been excited about as well. But he was not, quite the opposite. His only response was to tell me that the letters were not really from Hannah, and that someone was essentially playing a cruel joke on me. I did not want to hear that from him or anyone for that matter. Nobody believes me, you included, that the letters are actually coming from Hannah."

"And why do you think that is?"

"People want me to be unhappy."

"Why do you think people want you to be unhappy? What motivation would I possibly have to see you unhappy? And Ricky, he has been your best friend for how many years? Twenty-five? You have told me that he has always been there for you and has played a huge role in your life. What possible motivation could he have to seeing you unhappy?"

"I do not know, I am not in people's heads."

"I think you are smart enough to realize that people do not "have it out for you."

"Being smart is irrelevant, it's not going to bring Frannie or Hannah back. Nothing will. I am having trouble getting my arms around that fact. This life just keeps taking things from me. I feel beaten up, so it is only natural for me to question people's motivations."

"This is a completely normal reaction to what you have experienced. I often hear from people who have experienced losses like you have describe their moods as feeling beaten up.

Difficulty forgiving others, feelings of hopelessness, exhaustion, desires to isolate – these are all emotions I have had expressed to me. You are not alone. Have you given any thought to attending the support groups we spoke about? I think you could really benefit from doing so."

"I have a hard time understanding how it would be helpful to sit around and listen to a bunch of depressing stories about other children being lost. To me, this sounds like a breeding ground for cultivating deeper depression. I do not think that I am the only one suffering depression as the result of losing a child, but that does not mean I want to know about others' suffering."

"It is not so much about hearing from other people who have similar issues, the real benefit comes from hearing their stories of loss and recovery, and opening up and sharing what you have gone through. It can be very therapeutic to share your story with others who can relate."

"I just do not see how that would help, I'm sorry. I do not like talking about Frannie and Hannah at all, even with you. How am I going to open up to a room full of strangers?"

"Your hesitation and concern are both normal. But patients have generally told me that they find these sessions helpful, and that they have an easier time opening up when they are amongst strangers who can identify with their issues."

"Look, I do not think that is something I would be interested in. What is there to talk about or share? I am devastated, I am empty. My life without them is one of non-existence. I am simply floating through time, basically waiting to die."

"The power to change that lies within you Kenneth, it is there if you want it. I am not trying to downplay what you have gone through, not in the least, but you do not have to spend the rest of your life suffering. You can move on while still remembering and honoring Frannie and Hannah. You should not equate healing with forgetting, you can progress and begin to heal while still remembering them."

"I will give it some thought, happy? I am not promising anything."

Kenneth got up to leave as the session had come to an end. Dr. Kaplan extended his hand to Kenneth, saying that he was proud of him and that today's session was a good one.

CHAPTER XXII

Jennifer was very saddened by Kenneth's latest letter. She felt a strong connection to Kenneth, even though they had never met and Kenneth presumably had no idea who the letters from Hannah had actually been coming from. She wished there was some way she could help him but aside from writing more letters, she had no idea what to do. She could sense a marked decline in Kenneth's demeanor over the course of his past few letters, he did not do much to hide this. Jennifer was determined to make her next letter as upbeat as possible. With that in mind, she sat down and began writing.

May 5, 2015

Dear Daddy,

Mommy and me have the most wonderful tea parties! She dresses up like a queen and she dresses me up as a princess. I told her that I used to dress you up as a princess for our tea parties and she could not stop laughing.

I am sorry you had a bad experience at IHOP. Cheryl was a really nice lady, she always gave me extra whipped cream on my "funny-face" pancake. You shouldn't let that upset you, I want memories of me to make you happy, not sad. It should make you happy just like mint pistachio ice cream makes me happy, which I eat a lot of. The other day, me and Mommy were eating ice cream and it got all over her nose, boy did we laugh hard.

The pools here are really nice and the water is always warm. Mommy cannot believe how good I swim, I even showed her how good I hold my breath under water. She told me I look like a little fishy. Sometimes I swim with Mommy and sometimes I swim with my friends. You would also be proud of me if you saw me in the pool. There is a huge slide that puts you in the deep end. I went down it for the first time the other day and I loved it. I swam right towards the shallow end just like Nicole taught me. I am still playing a lot of kick ball and I am getting pretty good. I would like to play with you someday so you can see how far I can kick the ball.

The arts and crafts here are really great, there are like a million types of crayons, markers, paints, and clay. Me and my friends make projects every day. I usually make things for Mommy. I am so happy there are birds living in the bird house we made together, what are their names? I think one of their names should be Fred. What do they do for food? Do you feed them?

The zip line is my favorite activity still. I have been going down it a lot and landing in the ball pit. I know you do not like ball pits, but they are very clean here so Mommy said it was ok for me to go in them. Mommy even went down the

zip line a few times. She was scared and yelled out loud while

she was going down it.

I do all of these activities with Mommy or with Taylor,

Jordyn, and Laura. Taylor is a really good swimmer, she can

dive off the diving board! I have a lot of fun playing with

them. Laura and Taylor are both five and a half years old and

Jordyn is my age. We all get along really nicely. None of their

parents are here with them, I am the only one my age it seems

that has a mommy or daddy here. I feel very lucky to have

Mommy here with me. I am glad that Mommy is here with

me, especially because I get to sleep with her every night.

Why were you mean to Uncle Ricky? He is your best

friend. You always told me to be nice to people, especially

your friends. Was he mean to you first? I think it is important

to have friends, and I don't want you to be fighting with him.

Mommy agrees with me, and she also wants to know why you

were mean to him. She said he should be the most important part of your life now that me and Mommy are not with you. She was not happy that you were mean to him and said that you should tell him you are sorry. I get along really well with my friends here, we never fight over anything. Mommy says I play really nicely with everyone. Mommy has some friends here too, and she always gets along with them.

Daddy, I miss you a lot. I hope you know that. Mommy said to tell you that you need to try and find meaning in your life, and from that, you will find happiness again. I don't really know what that means, but if Mommy says it, it must be true. Be happy. Smile. If you have trouble smiling, just think of me and Mommy. I love you.

Love,
Princess Hannah

CHAPTER XXIII

Kenneth took Hannah's letter to heart, and set out to make amends with Ricky. He called him on his cell phone and asked if he could meet him for lunch. Ricky reluctantly agreed to meet Kenneth at a café near Ricky's office at noon. This gave Kenneth ample time to prepare for an excursion into the outside world, both physically and mentally. Kenneth shaved for the first time in weeks, showered, and changed into something other than sweat pants.

He arrived at the café a few minutes early so he could ensure they got a table in the back, this way they could have some degree of privacy. Kenneth felt that he could earn back Ricky's trust if he just showed up and presented an honest face, instead of his usual grimace. Ricky showed up at noon, he was wearing a suit as he had come straight from work. After Kenneth ordered a soda and Ricky ordered a sandwich, Ricky wasted no time.

"Let me start out by saying that although you are my best friend, if you talk to me like you did last time, I am going to get up and leave, no questions asked."

"Understood, and let me apologize for the way our last encounter went. That was not me yelling at you, that was the bourbon."

"You cannot go through life blaming everything on alcohol. If that's your MO, then you'd better start attending some AA meetings or check yourself into rehab or something."

"I do not need AA or rehab."

"You certainly have me fooled."

"It may have been the bourbon that caused me to yell at

you, but I feel that I had a legitimate reason for getting upset."

"This is not going to be another conversation about the letters you have been receiving, is it?"

"Why is it so hard to believe that somehow, Hannah is reaching out to me from another place? Maybe she is in a special place just for children where such communications are possible."

"Again, do you hear what you are saying?"

"I hear exactly what I am saying. But I did not call you to discuss the letters. I wanted to apologize to you, which I did. I also just wanted to shoot the shit like we used to. Tell me about the kids, how is Jules doing? How old are the boys now? How is work?"

"How old are the boys Kenneth? You have not been away for years. The boys are still five and three, the same age as the last time you saw them. Jules is doing fine, work is fine. All is fine by me. I am just extremely worried about you."

"You needn't be. I am fine. I am better than fine."

"You planning on going back to work at some point?"

"I have not thought about it, money is the least of my worries."

"I'm not asking because of money. I'm asking from the standpoint of you reentering society, having some sort of purpose again."

"Your idea of having purpose is for me to bill 75 hours a week, be inundated with work, have "immediate" deadlines thrust upon me, and listening to brainless partners making mundane criticisms of my work, all in the hopes of one day being named a partner of a firm I do not give a damn about, and that does not give a damn about me? That is no longer my purpose, and quite frankly, I'm not sure it ever was."

"So then what are your plans Kenneth, sweatpants, bourbon, and take-out food for the rest of your life? That is not a life brother. That is barely an existence."

"I do not know what my plan is Ricky. You want to know the real truth, take a look in my eyes. Do you see anything there? Because I do not. And it is not for a lack of looking, I spend hours every day looking in the mirror trying to find something there. Maybe if I look long enough, it will appear. Like one of those old "magic" posters where you had to "unfocus" your eyes and you would then see the hidden sailboat or spaceship. I have tried to unfocus, for hours on end, but all I see are two vacant eyes looking back at me. There is nothing there.

You know what sticks with me? The other day I passed a car that had a bumper sticker that read "how quickly will your joy pass?" It felt like the bumper sticker was talking directly to me. And then it felt a bit presumptuous, what business did this bumper sticker have in assuming I felt any joy to begin with? I got past this though, because I realized that I do have joy. Every time I receive a letter from Hannah and every time I respond to her, the emotion I feel is joy.

Fleeting it may be, but it is joy nonetheless. However, I am

filled with this constant fear that these little slices of joy

sandwiched between much thicker slices of misery will

someday be ripped from me. And then I saw that bumper

sticker, and it was something more than fate. It was speaking

directly at me. It confirmed that feeling of dread that follows

me around like a fucking shadow, the feeling that this joy is

only temporary. Are you following me?"

Ricky did not quite know how to respond to this. To

him, this sounded like the ramblings of a possibly drunk man

who was teetering on the very brisk of insanity. He realized

that this was dangerous territory for his best friend, and he

did not want to say the wrong thing which would lead to a

similar outcome as their last meeting.

"Do you feel you deserve joy?" Ricky asked.

"No. Not at all."

"Why not?"

"I am here, living a life of misery, if you can even call it a life. My wife and daughter are gone, both dying well before their time while I continue on this nightmare trip. Why should I be rewarded for that?"

"It is not about being rewarded. It is about cherishing the fact that you are alive and here to carry on Frannie and Hannah's legacies."

"I do not feel like I am carrying on any legacies at all. I am essentially going through the motions, waiting for my turn to die so I can see my girls again."

"Have you expressed these feelings to your therapist?"

"Maybe not in the detail we discussed today, but I think I have told him the gist of it."

"Does he know about the letters?"

"I have talked to him about them. His reaction was largely negative. Not so much taking the position that the letters were not really from Hannah, but he expressed concern over what will happen if and when they stop coming."

"Do you have a response to that? What will you do if they stop coming?"

"I honestly do not know, I try not to think about it. It is easier for me to visualize my continuing to receive them and the joy that accompanies them. And I try to ignore all the doubters of the letters' authenticity, unfortunately, present company included."

"Kenneth, we have been best friends for more than twenty years. We have both gotten each other out of some pretty tight jams. You were there for me when my first marriage failed, I was there for you when Frannie passed and to the extent you allowed me, when Hannah passed as well. But you are in a rut right now that has me stumped. I do not know how to guide you. I think you need help, or more help than you have been getting. I do not think seeing a therapist once every week or two is going to cut it."

"Dr. Kaplan recommended that I seek out and attend support groups for people who have experienced losses like I have."

"I think that is a great idea." Ricky enthusiastically responded.

"I do not know about that. Like I said to him, isn't that just going to bring me down more to hear horror stories of other young children dying well before their time?"

"I am not a doctor, but it sounds like something that could have a therapeutic benefit for you. It will provide you a forum to express a lot of the bad feelings you have been experiencing with people who will understand what you are going through."

"I will look into it."

"Promise?"

"I said I will."

And with that, their lunch came to an end. Ricky picked up the tab, for which Kenneth expressed his gratitude. Ricky hugged his best friend tightly, told him he was proud of him, and went on his way back to work. Kenneth stayed at the café for a bit mulling over his conversation with Ricky. After about half an hour, Kenneth got up to leave, with his home as his intended destination.

CHAPTER XXIV

The next morning Kenneth flipped on the computer for the first time in a while, he had stopped checking e-mail a long time ago. There were only so many "my condolences" e-mails he could take, and he reached that limit pretty quickly. Sure, everyone meant well, but they did not realize how much these e-mails hurt, each one feeling like a dagger in his heart. His goal was to conduct some research into loss support groups in the Brighton area. He still was not sure if he wanted to go down this road, but he figured there was no harm in seeing what was out there.

He went to Google's homepage, intentionally bypassing his e-mail which was usually his first step along the "information superhighway." He typed in "loss support groups Brighton" into the search field, which yielded 749,000 results. He knew there was a way to use the advanced search feature to narrow down the field of results, but he did not have the motivation for that. He instead read through the first few results that came up. It turned out that there were a few appropriate groups in the Brighton area, so he went with the first one that came up, the Brighton Loss Recovery Support Group, or the BLRSG.

The BLRSG met every other Tuesday at a local church. According to the website, the next meeting was tomorrow night. The moderator of the group was a man named Jack Roberts, for whom there was an "About Me" page on the website. Apparently, Jack had lost both his children, ages eight and five, coincidentally during a fatal car accident nearly seven years ago. He was married and recently his wife gave birth to a baby girl named Riley. Whereas at first Kenneth felt a connection to Jack due to the car accident scenarios, he then felt a strong disconnect due to the fact that he still had a wife and was able to have another child. Kenneth felt resentment towards this stranger, albeit unjustifiably.

The next day, Kenneth did not get dressed until 6:00 pm. He threw on a pair of jeans and a tee shirt, took two swigs of bourbon and a Klonopin, and headed out to the meeting. Upon his arrival, he was greeted by none other than Jack Roberts. Kenneth introduced himself and Jack thanked him for coming. Kenneth helped himself to a complimentary cup of coffee and sat down among a cross-section of people. The chairs were in a circular formation with a podium facing the circle. As the meeting got underway, there were about fourteen people present, including Jack and Kenneth. Jack stood at the podium and made his opening remarks:

"Good evening and welcome to this evening's meeting of the Brighton Loss Recovery Support group. We have some newcomers this evening, would you care to introduce yourselves?"

"Hi, my name is Kenneth Hill," Kenneth said quietly when it came around to him.

Jack continued: "For those of you who are new to the BLRSG, welcome. This is a very good and supportive group of people, so there is really no reason to feel scared or uncomfortable. Nobody is ever forced to share if they do not want to. There are very few rules, but the ones we do have are very important. Rule #1 is that everything that is shared here, stays here. Being able to share in confidence is the cornerstone of the program and ensures that the group is successful. Rule #2 is that there is no cross-talking, it is very rude and disruptive to the person speaking. Rule #3 is that there are absolutely no criticisms or negative comments directed to anyone sharing. Positive comments are of course welcomed and encouraged. And finally, Rule #4 is that there is no complaining about the coffee, it is free. So who would like to get us started?"

A woman sitting next to Kenneth raised her hand. She appeared to be in her late forties, neatly but casually dressed. She approached the podium and Jack took a seat next to it. She seemed very serious as she approached, as if she was guarding something within herself. After introducing herself as Denise from Brighton, she began her tale:

"Our only daughter, Emily, was a good kid. She got good grades, played on a bunch of sports teams, had lots of friends, was generally well-liked by everyone. When she was accepted into a number of Ivy League schools, we were ecstatic. Particularly because several of the acceptances had been accompanied by scholarship offers. [This last comment eliciting some laughter from the audience]. She decided on Brown University after touring a number of schools, because she felt "most at home" at Brown. Thankfully, Brown was also the one that came through with a full scholarship offer, otherwise we were not sure how we were going to pay for her schooling.

The first semester was a dream, with her ending up with a 3.7 GPA and making Dean's list. She came home frequently on weekends, excitedly telling us about professors she got to meet and classes she got to take. She was soaking in all that Brown had to offer and we could not be more pleased. Her second semester was more of the same, finishing her freshman year with a 3.75 GPA.

The first semester of her sophomore year was when things began to change. The first thing we noticed was that she stopped calling us every day as she used to, and her visits home became spaced further apart. When she did come home, the topics of conversation were less about professors and classes and more about new friends she had made and parties she had gone to. She did not want to see her friends from home, preferring instead to do her laundry, see some of her friends from Brown, and get back to school. She seemed edgy and anxious, not the calm, collected, positive girl we had always known. Perhaps these should have all been warning signs to us, but we chalked it up to the "college experience."

However, we had a harder time digesting her 1.7 GPA that semester, which put her in danger of losing her scholarship. She explained that she had taken a lot of really tough classes that semester, and curiously, that a number of her professors "had it out for her." When we pressed her on this issue, she could not give any justification for this paranoia. We found out, later on, that she hardly went to any of her classes and walked out of two of her final exams. She apologized for the GPA and assured us that she would get her grades back up the following semester. We believed her.

It was only six weeks later that we got the phone call. It was 7:00 pm on an otherwise quiet Wednesday night when we received a phone call from the Rhode Island Hospital saying that Emily was very ill and that we needed to come to the hospital immediately. Upon our arrival, we were pulled into a conference room by a doctor who did not look a day over twenty-one. His demeanor was nothing but somber. Apparently, Emily had overdosed on a cocktail of cocaine and crystal methamphetamine. "Not our Emily" was out first response, she hated drugs and the people who used them. The doctor assured us it was her. She was presently in a coma, essentially being kept alive by machines. Even if she were to wake up, the doctor said, she would no doubt have suffered severe brain damage due to an extended lack of oxygen to her brain.

We were escorted to Emily's room by the nurses, and were stopped dead in our tracks when we saw her. She was frail, having lost significant weight since we last saw her. She was so pale she was nearly transparent. There were tubes and

IVs littering her body, and I will never forget the sound of the ventilator keeping her alive. I remember kissing her cold and sweaty forehead, telling her that "mommy and daddy were there to make it all better." My husband and I sat by her bed all night, each of us holding her cold hands. Emily passed away at 6:47 am the next morning, with my husband and I still holding her hands.

This was two years ago. My husband and I have since divorced, never being able to come to terms with each other's blindness and ignorance to Emily's situation. Not a day goes by that I do not think about Emily. Not a day goes by that I do not think about the warning signs that were plainly visible to see. But we were like ostriches hiding our heads in the sand. We believed that Emily was too smart to befriend any drug abusers, let alone to start abusing drugs herself. That thought just never crossed our minds, and in hindsight, it should have. We were naïve, we were stupid, we were stubborn, we were simply clueless.

People try to console me by saying that there was nothing we could have done. This is not comforting in the least because it is not accurate. There was plenty we could have done, we just ignored that which was plain to see. And we paid, or rather Emily paid the ultimate price for our inaction. Emily is no longer here because of me. My precious baby who was going to change the world is gone because I chose not to see. I killed my baby girl. I still have nightmares every night of her lying in that hospital bed, the feel of her cold hands. She never awoke from the coma and we never got a chance to say goodbye. I think that is the hardest part, I never had an opportunity to tell her how much I loved her. Or to tell her I was proud of her. Or simply to brush her beautiful hair behind her ear and reassure her that all would be ok.

I failed my baby, and every day since has been a living nightmare. I can never forgive myself, no do I want to. I do not deserve forgiveness. I do not deserve happiness. I do not deserve respect. I deserve exactly what I am now the recipient of – guilt, shame, and misery.

Thank you for listening to me."

Denise sat down in her chair and Jack went back up to the podium. "I want to thank Denise for sharing her story, it was a very touching story and we are grateful for your sharing it." Everyone in the audience agreed and thanked her, everyone except Kenneth. Jack continued: "I will now open the floor for comments or questions."

"I think that was a very powerful story," said a man who introduced himself as Jerry, "and I thank you for sharing. The only part I had a problem with was your saying you do not deserve forgiveness or respect. I disagree. As far as forgiveness, you should understand that you did not do anything wrong warranting forgiveness. It sounds like Emily was not under your control when this happened; rather she was under control of the drugs. It does not sound like you could have done anything. As far as not deserving respect, I think you deserve all the respect in the world. First off, it sounds like you were a great parent to Emily and loved her very much. Second, it took a lot of courage and fortitude to tell your story here to a group full of strangers. For that, you deserve our respect. I can only speak for myself, but you earned my respect."

Jack stood at the podium and thanked Jerry for his thoughtful and honest response. He asked if anyone else had any feedback and the room was quiet. "Ok, so no one wants to share anything with Denise? Going once, going twice, gone." Jack quipped. "Thank you again Denise. Who would like to share next?"

"I'll go" responded the man sitting next to Kenneth. The man was dressed in a suit and tie, looking like he had just come from work. Kenneth was unsure if he felt like sharing his story with a room full of strangers, so he was happy this other man volunteered. He walked up to the podium and began speaking: "Hello everyone, my name is Jason, thank you for letting me attend the meeting tonight. I thought Denise's story was very touching; I'm not nearly as eloquent or articulate as she is, so my story will be a lot briefer.

I lost my wife six months ago to breast cancer. It was a fairly quick progression from diagnosis to death. She was my first and only love, we were high school sweethearts. We have a two year old daughter who will never know her mother. We had been together for seventeen years, married for nine. I don't know how to live without her. I don't know what it means to be an independent person; I only know what it's like to be one half of a couple. We were always just Jason and Sara, the couple whose sum was greater than its parts.

I know I have to keep it together for our daughter, I am all that she has. But I am finding it so difficult. Thankfully, I have been getting a lot of assistance from both sets of grandparents. It has essentially allowed me time to grieve, which is all I seem to do. I have been unable to work in any capacity. I feel so empty. A friend of mine asked if I wanted to be set-up with one of his co-workers, but the thought of being with another woman aside from Sara was so foreign to me that I looked at him like he had four heads. Without her, I am not a person. I am simply a shadow of my former self, going through the motions, waiting for an opportunity to see her again. I cannot even be a father, that is how paralyzing my grief is. Every time I hear my daughter say "mama," I absolutely lose it. As poor a father as I am, she is the only thing that has prevented me from putting a gun in my mouth."

And with that last comment, Jason began to sob at the podium. There was an awkward silence that came over the room, broken only by a loud snicker from Kenneth. Kenneth stood up and began to angrily speak from his seat in lieu of going to the podium: "You people do not know anything about loss. What have I heard here tonight? A story about a junkie and a grown woman passing who had the opportunity to live a good chunk of her life."

Denise stood up and angrily shouted in return: "my daughter was not a junkie."

"No?" said Kenneth. "What would you call a person who could not limit her intake of heavy drugs, to the point of overdosing? I would call that a junkie. She knew the path she was on and continued on it until it killed her. You say that she was here to change the world, but she obviously had other plans. I do not doubt that you loved her and are sad about her passing, but it could have been avoided if you had in fact paid more attention to the warning signs."

"You do not know what pain is," Kenneth continued. "Pain is losing a spouse to cancer and then shortly thereafter, while still in the grieving process, losing your five year old daughter during a car crash perpetrated by a drunk driver. Pain is seeing that other driver walking away from that crash unscathed while your toddler lie motionless, still buckled into her car seat. Pain is having the EMT on the scene telling you that your five year old daughter is dead. Pain is walking around every day knowing that you survived the crash and she did not. Pain is thinking that if we had just left the movie theater one minute earlier or later, Hannah would still be here today." Now it was Kenneth's turn to sob.

Jack walked over to the podium, feeling a bit stunned at the exchange that had just occurred. "Thank you Jason for sharing your story about Sara, and I am sorry for your loss. Kenneth is it? I said at the beginning of the meeting that cross-talk and disparaging remarks were not permitted. You failed to adhere to both rules; while I am deeply sorry for your losses, I am afraid I am going to have to ask you to leave.

Thank you for joining us here tonight and goodbye."

Kenneth made for the exit, feeling even worse than when he had come in. Although it was late, he called Dr. Kaplan and left a message saying that he needed to come in. He headed home, knowing there was a bottle of bourbon, plenty of pills, and a pad of paper waiting for him.

CHAPTER XXV

Kenneth arrived home from the support group at approximately 9:30 pm, intent on writing a letter to Hannah. There was a message on the answering machine from his father, Michael. His mother, Christine, had passed away many years ago from lung cancer, smoking her Camels right up to the very end. Michael wanted to know when he was going to see Kenneth, as it had been almost a month since his last visit.

Kenneth's father was in his late 70s and in good health. Kenneth had always had a good relationship with his father. His father lived in a nearby suburb, not far from either Kenneth or Barry. Michael had a good relationship with Lucy, Barry and Michele as well; Kenneth was just typically

Michael's first call when he needed something. The death of Kenneth's mother hit Michael very hard, they had been married for thirty-six years and did everything together. She was generally the one who managed their friends and social calendar, essentially wearing the hat of event coordinator. When she passed, Michael's "couples" friendships slowly began to taper off. Not entirely unlike what had happened to Kenneth's friendships when Frannie passed. Not to say that Michael's friends were not there for him when Christine passed, because they were, he just was not great at staying in touch with people.

Kenneth felt bad that he had not seen his father since Alex's party and made it a point to call him back tomorrow and set a time to go over there. In the meantime, he wanted to write Hannah. He went into the kitchen and took a Klonopin, using bourbon to chase it down. He then finished the glass of bourbon and poured himself a second glass, which he took to his "office." He sat down at his desk and began to write while

sipping his drink.

June 11, 2015

Dear Princess Hannah,

How is my favorite girl doing? Thank you for your

most recent letter. To answer your question, Mommy always

loved vanilla chip ice cream. There was a time before you

were born that Mommy and I were walking along the

boardwalk eating ice cream cones. I asked her if I could have a

taste of hers, she said yes and held up her cone for me to take

a lick. When I went to taste it, she mushed the cone right into

my nose! She laughed and laughed the most beautiful laugh. I

really miss Mommy a lot.

It sounds like you are doing a lot of fun activities. I am

glad to hear that you get to swim, I am sure that Mommy is so

impressed with how good you are. I know Nicole misses you

a lot. Kick ball also sounds like a lot of fun, I bet that you can kick the ball very far. The zip line sounds SO cool, I wish I could see you and Mommy going down it. Mommy is ok landing in the ball pit? What types of arts and crafts do you make for Mommy? I still have all of your arts and crafts projects on your "Projects Wall of Fame" in your bedroom. My favorite is still the picture you drew of you, Mommy, and me at the beach, you drew all of us so well.

You and Mommy will be happy to know that I told Ricky that I was sorry for being mean. He accepted my apology and things are ok. I realized that he cares a lot about me and was just trying to look out for me. That is what friends do for one another. I am glad that you get along so well with Laura, Jordyn, and Taylor. They sound like really nice girls. It is important to have friends who care about you, and that you care about in return.

I am going to see Poppy tomorrow. He is doing well, he

just misses you and Mommy a lot. You used to have so much fun playing with him. Remember when he used to take you fishing? You two would laugh and laugh as you dropped the worms as you tried to put them on the hooks. You loved to pick the worms up and then wipe your hands on Poppy's jeans. I will never forget the size of the fish you caught, although you would not taste it after Poppy grilled it and ate it for dinner that night. You said it made the whole house stink!

Ok pumpkin, I am going to finish this letter because I am tired. I love and miss you tons.

Love,
Daddy

Kenneth sat back in his chair, feeling a little bit guilty that this letter was so short. There just was not a lot to write about; a detailed description of his misery was certainly not appropriate for a letter to a five year old. He finished his second glass of bourbon, and feeling the effects of the

Klonopin, headed upstairs to pass out.

CHAPTER XXVI

The next day, Kenneth made the fifteen minute drive to his father's home for the first time in a month. His father had been a widower for more than ten years, but he was not one to wallow in his misery. Kenneth apparently did not pick up that trait. Michael was in his late 70s, went to the gym every day, and still played in his weekly card game with his friends every Thursday night.

He and Kenneth had always been close, having both lost a spouse brought them even closer together. Kenneth had chosen the same career path as his father in the field of law, and had lived a life that closely paralleled his father's. Lucy married young and became a housewife, giving birth to her first child at a very young age. Barry chose a more creative path, and had enjoyed a fair degree of success as an artist. He married Michele, who was a "stay-at-home" mom like Lucy to children Alex and Stacey. Before Barry had achieved his success, he and Michele were forced to move back into Barry's parents' house. Now they live in a huge home in the suburbs, his success as an artist affording them many of life's finer pleasures. He was not spoiled by his success, though, and would gladly give you the shirt off his back, even during times he could not afford another one.

Kenneth arrived at his father's house around 11:00 am, figuring they would have lunch together, notwithstanding Kenneth's lack of appetite.

"Hello son." Michael greeted him at the door.

"Hey Pop." Kenneth responded as he entered his childhood home, always finding it much smaller than he had remembered it growing up.

"How's my boy doing?"

Kenneth thought for a minute before answering this question. "I'm not doing so great Pop."

"Come in and sit down, we can talk it out just like we used to. I got you through the Bar Exam, didn't I? What can I get you to drink?"

"Got any bourbon?" Kenneth half-jokingly asked.

"I hope you are kidding, it is 11:00 in the morning."

"I was," said Kenneth, gauging his father's reaction first. "I'll just take a bottle of water." He was not going to publicize that he was already two glasses of bourbon into the day.

His father went into the kitchen to get Kenneth a bottle of water while Kenneth sat down in the living room. He looked at a picture of his mother that was on the living room table. She had been a beautiful woman, even right up to the end of her life. He could see a little bit of Hannah in her, the same eyes and blond hair. It was at that moment that he realized just how much he missed his mother, and made the startling connection that all the women in his life left him prematurely.

"Do you miss mom?" Kenneth began when his father sat down on the couch adjacent to him.

"Every day. What makes you ask?"

"I have been thinking of Frannie a lot lately and I am not sure why."

"You are human, that is why."

"Mom passed away what, twelve years ago? You still think of her every day?"
Kenneth asked, sounding surprised.

"Of course I do. I spent the majority of my life with that woman. We laughed together, we cried together, we danced together, we grieved losses together. Not a day goes by that I do not hear the wind call out your mother's name. She was my everything, if you told me that you did not still think of

Frannie all the time, I would tell you that something was

wrong with you. I know you have been through several

variations of hell, more than anyone should have to endure in

a lifetime. You are entitled and expected to think of and grieve

for the people, the women you have lost in your lifetime.

People who say that time heals all wounds are people who

have not experienced true loss in their lifetimes. Time does not

heal all wounds, it just dulls the senses so the wounds become

more tolerable. The truth is, you do not want the wounds to

heal. To heal means to forget, and I do not want to forget. Not

everyone may agree with that sentiment, but it is truly how I

feel."

"I do not want to forget, I do not want to heal. I agree

that in the process of healing, I will be forced to forget about

them. I do not want that."

"And I think that is a valid means of living, and a valid

way to keep Frannie and Hannah's place in your heart consistent."

"What is your status with returning to work?" Michael continued.

"I still have no desire to return to work. The last I spoke with my the firm, they said that my position would remain open for as long as I needed."

"You know that type of good will is going to have a shelf life. Eventually, business and the almighty dollar will overcome compassion. It is not in the firm's interest to keep that offer open to you indefinitely."

"But my work product was always well-received, I was always well-liked there."

"That may be true, but you have not worked since Hannah left us, you do not know what it is going to be like when you get back, if you go back. If you return, they are not going to tolerate inconsistency from you. Remember, you will still just be a cog in the wheel that can be easily replaced. The last thing you need is to be permanently unemployed on top of everything else you are going through."

"I know. As it stands, I don't know if and when I would go back. Right now, I cannot bring myself to think about it."

"I understand and think you are justified, but you are going to have to come up with some sort of a game plan. When was the last time you were in touch with them?"

"I spoke with HR about two weeks ago, they called to check in on me. The firm also sent me a basket from Edible Arrangements last week."

"That's swell. What did HR say?"

"Nothing in particular. Asked how I was feeling. I was honest with them and told him them I am not doing great. I told them that Hannah's passing has had a tremendous impact on me. They said they understood."

"And?"

"And they asked if I had any plans to return."

"There it is. Do not let their apparent sympathy and fruit baskets fool you. They are a business and they have a business to run. At the moment, you are not benefiting them at all, you are not working, billing hours, and pulling in revenue for the firm. They are trying to gauge if and when you are going to return so they know when they can expect to start making money off you again. Remember, at the moment, they are essentially paying you for nothing in return. Think about your co-workers who picked up your slack, your caseload once you left," Michael continued, "their workloads were probably a lot heavier as a result. And with their added work, not everyone's productivity necessarily increased in conjunction. They want you back for business purposes, not because you are a good guy. I do no mean to sound harsh, I am just being realistic as someone who has been in their shoes

before. I know I have said it before, but it is worth repeating –
the goodwill will run out eventually, everyone has a breaking
point."

"I know Pop. I can see myself going back at some point,
I just do not know when." Kenneth did not really believe that,
but he figured it would be a good way to get his father off his
back and segue into a different topic.

"So what else is going on?" Michael asked. "How have
you been feeling?"

"Not great. I cannot get Hannah out of my head."

"Nobody is asking or expecting you to get her out of
your head. Like I said, it will get easier over time."

"I DON'T WANT IT TO GET EASIER." Kenneth
shouted at his father, a very rare occurrence. "I want to hurt, I
want to feel, I do not want to stop thinking about her. I feel
that once I stop doing all those things, it will be like Hannah
was never even here."

"That is not the case son, that is not how it works. You can get better and heal, but you can also honor, remember, and love her. Turn the tables a little bit. If you were Hannah, would you want to know that your Dad was spending his whole life being miserable and suffering? Or would you want to know that he was getting his life back on track, honoring and missing you, but moving onwards?"

"The latter, obviously, makes more sense logically. But it is so much easier said than done. I do not see myself being able to accomplish that. I just cannot process Hannah's passing. The driver of the other car is sitting in prison, but at least he is still alive. He did not lose anything. He does not wake up every day with a horrendous, empty pit in his stomach. He does not spend his days wondering when he will see his baby girl again. Eventually, he will get out of prison and be free to live his life again. Where is the justice in that?"

"There is no justice in that, you are right. But whether

he was given the death penalty or spends the rest of his life in prison would not bring Hannah back to you, would it? So what good does it do for you to spend even five seconds thinking about him? I will answer it for you, none. Focus on what matters, which is trying to get to a place where you can think of Frannie and Hannah in a positive light, not a negative one, get back to work, and move on with your life."

"I do not know how to do that."

"Have you looked into or tried and of the loss support groups we spoke about? Sometimes they can be helpful."

"I did go to one, but it was a disaster. I was actually asked to leave."

"Why?"

"Because of my "disruptive behavior," I just could not bear to hear other people's stories that seemed to pale in comparison to my own. One woman talked about losing her college-aged daughter to drugs and a man shared who had lost his wife to cancer. The stories seemed so trite to me, and I made it a point to tell them that."

"Kenneth, I am disappointed in you. First off, that is not how I raised you. You were raised to be respectful to people, regardless of how you feel inside. Second, how were their stories much different than yours? A woman lost her child like you and a man lost his wife just like you did."

"The woman did not lose a child like me." Kenneth could feel himself getting angry. "She lost a grown daughter who essentially chose death by overdosing on drugs. That girl had an opportunity to live a good portion of her life, and it was her own poor decisions that squandered her opportunities. That is nothing like Hannah. Hannah was only five, and had barely lived any part of her life. Her death was brought upon us by the negligent acts of another, not by any conscious decision of her own.

I suppose the man's story about losing his wife to

cancer was similar to my own, I think it was just the visualization of such a similar story combined with the woman's story that just set me off. In hindsight, I know I was wrong. At the time, I just got so angry."

"Had you been drinking before the meeting?"

"I don't remember. It is likely."

"How are things going with the psychologist?"

Kenneth was very close with his father, so he had not kept the fact that he had been seeing a psychologist from him. "It is going ok I guess. He spends most of the time talking about Hannah's passing and how I feel about it. I do not know what he expects to hear. It devastated me, it tore my heart out. I have expressed to him that I wish it would have been me that was killed, not Hannah."

"And what good would that have done? Then you would have a five year old with no parents, who would become a ward of the state. That is unless your brother or sister stepped up to raise her, which I am sure is not what you would want."

"But she would be alive. She had her whole life ahead of her, and she would have gotten a chance to fulfill that. She was such a bright little girl, she could have grown up to do anything she wanted. She was robbed of all that."

"We are going around in circles. I do not mind talking about this, you know that, but I do not feel like we are getting anywhere."

"It helps to vent to you, even if the outcome is the same every time. It is good for me to verbalize these things, and I appreciate your listening."

"You are my son, you do not have to thank me for listening, it is what I am here for. I just want to see you turn your life around a bit."

Kenneth had agonized over the decision as to whether or not he should share the news of Hannah's letters with his father. So far, everyone that he had told about the letters had essentially called him crazy, not one person believed him. He thought it might be different with his father because of their close relationship. He decided to share the news with him, even if it meant one more person thinking he was crazy.

"Pop, there is something I have to tell you. It is a bit of a sensitive topic, so I want your honest opinion as to whether you believe me or not."

"You are gay." Michael said, trying to lighten the mood a little bit.

"No, Pop, I am not gay. I have been receiving letters from Hannah. It began as an exercise my therapist had me doing, writing letters to Hannah as a means to help my recovery. I took a shot, I still do not know why, at mailing them to Hannah in Heaven. You can imagine my surprise when I received a letter back from her. Since then, we have written each other four or five times."

Like Ricky and Dr. Kaplan before him, Kenneth's father was a bit taken aback and took a little bit of time to respond. Indeed, he was not quite sure how to respond. His initial, gut reaction was to tell Kenneth that he had lost it. But he was wise enough to know that he had to tread carefully around this one. He decided to ignore his initial reaction and see where the conversation went.

"What did Hannah have to say?" Michael finally asked.

"She is not in any pain, she is having a lot of fun where she is. Frannie found her when she arrived, and they have been spending a lot of time together. In fact, Hannah gets to sleep with Frannie every night. She has made a few really good friends with whom she plays with regularly. She plays a lot of dress-up, kick ball, and swimming. She said Frannie was very excited to see her swim, something she never got a chance to do before she passed. Hannah also talks a lot about a zip line that drops you off in a ball pit.

All in all, it sounds like she is doing very well, I am happy to hear that neither her nor Frannie are in any kind of pain. She seems to be having a lot of fun. To say that receiving these letters is my driving force to living is an understatement. I truly live for receiving her letters."

"Do you think that is healthy?" Asked Kenneth's father somewhat skeptically.

"How do you mean?"

"Referring back to the healing process we spoke of earlier. I am no psychologist, but if you continue having her as a pen pal, I feel like you are never going to be able to accept the fact that she is gone and start moving on with your life. You are never going to be able to heal."

"I already told you I do not want to let go. I do not want to lose her a second time. You really do not have any liquor in the house?" Kenneth asked as he began to sweat and nervously rock in his seat.

"No, I do not. Do you have a drinking problem that I now have to worry about as well?"

"No, I just feel like I could use a drink."

"Well, you are not getting one here, so deal with it. Tell me more about these letters from Hannah. What else, if anything, does she write to you?"

Kenneth was a little taken aback by the question. His father was the first person he had told about the letters that did not instantly question both the authenticity of the letters and his sanity. He was pleasantly surprised.

"She talks a lot about the time she spends with Frannie. So not only am I happy to be conversing with Hannah, but I am happy that she is getting to spend a lot of missed time with Frannie as well."

"How is it that Hannah, who was five years old when she was taken from us, reads and comprehends your letters and has the ability to write back?"

"Hannah said that Frannie helps her with those tasks."

"And how frequently do these letters get exchanged?"

"About every month or two. She usually urges me to reach out to Ricky, and to do things that will bring me happiness."

"And do you listen to her? Do you do things that make you happy?"

"That's a tough question to answer since there really is not much that makes me happy anymore. I enjoy receiving her letters. I do not see or hear from friends much anymore, Frannie was generally the one who made our plans and kept our social calendar filled in. Ricky and I are not on the best of terms, I did not particularly care for his reaction to my news of the letter writing. Him and I have not spoken much since then, and I only saw him one time since. During that visit, he again questioned the authenticity of the letters. I do not want or need that kind of negativity in my life. Other than that, I do not do much."

"Do you make it to the gym at all, or just sit home, get drunk, and wallow in your misery all day?"

"Probably more the latter." Kenneth said sheepishly.

"That does not make me happy. You are wasting away, both physically and mentally. You need to make some real changes Kenneth, or you will lose everything."

"I have already lost everything, what else is there to lose?"

"I can still lose YOU, you are still a person, my son, and I do not want to lose you."

"I love you Pop. Thanks for the talk." And with that, Kenneth asked if his father needed anything fixed around the house, light bulbs needing changing etc. His father responded in the negative. Kenneth hugged and kissed his father goodbye and made for the front door.

"Stay well son, like I used to tell you, keep your eye on

the ball and this too shall pass." Although they hugged

goodbye, his father would have hugged him just a little bit

longer if he knew that this would be the last time he would

ever see Kenneth alive.

CHAPTER XXVII

It was a little after 2:00 pm when Kenneth left his

father's home. He had an appointment with Dr. Kaplan at 4:00

pm, so he had two hours or so to kill. He headed straight for a

bar that was halfway in between his father's home and Dr.

Kaplan's office. He had an innate ability to find bars, not

exactly a desirable quality, but one he was skilled at

nonetheless.

It only took him a few minutes to get to the bar, a place

he had been on a few prior occasions. He walked in and took

an empty stool at the bar, there being only two other people in

the establishment. Apparently, 2:00 pm on weekdays was not

a busy time for bars. He ordered a bourbon, straight with no ice, and ordered a second one when the first one was delivered. The first one he downed in one gulp, with the second one being placed in front of him just as he finished the first. He nursed the second one a little bit longer.

The bartender attempted to make conversation with Kenneth, but Kenneth was simply uninterested. He was not trying to be rude, he just preferred to sit in silence with his drink and his thoughts. He had a productive visit with his father; Kenneth was pleased that his father did not pass judgment on his pen pal ship with Hannah. Everyone else has. To him, it was perfectly reasonable and was turning out to be quite therapeutic for him. He felt very bad that his last letter to Hannah was so short, he hoped that she would not hold it against him and would continue to write him.

As he sat there drinking his second bourbon, he felt a twang of emotional pain that jarred him. He missed Hannah more than normal, but he was unable to process the reason behind this. It was her laugh more than anything. She had a smile and laugh that would light up a room. It occurred to him that he had hardly smiled or laughed since Hannah passed. He felt no reason to. It was almost as if it would be disrespectful to Hannah if he did, he had no business experiencing happiness if Frannie and Hannah never again would. He regularly replayed the night of Hannah's death in his head, the things he could have done differently that might have prevented her death. Those recurring thoughts robbed his heart of any lasting joy.

He took out a Klonopin from his pocket and swallowed it down with the remainder of the second bourbon. He paid his tab and left the bar, heading for Dr. Kaplan's office. The irony of his getting behind the wheel of a car after he had been drinking was not lost on him, but he was too entrenched in his misery to avoid it. Besides, finding a time when he had no bourbon in his system was not easy, with his complete sobriety becoming a scarce commodity.

He arrived at Dr. Kaplan's office about twenty minutes after leaving the bar. He was right on time for his appointment and Dr. Kaplan took him right in.

"Are you drunk?" Dr. Kaplan asked in somewhat of an accusatory manner.

"No." Kenneth replied.

"Have you been drinking?"

"Yes, I had a few drinks, but I am ok to go ahead with the session."

"Kenneth, you reek of alcohol. You are lucky you did not get pulled over."

"Can we change the topic please?"

"Fine, I just want to make sure you are coherent enough to proceed with the session."

"I. Am. Fine."

"Ok, I will not bring it up again. How have you been

doing?"

"With the exception of the letters from Hannah, not good. I feel like a ghost who is walking around looking for something. I feel like a non-entity. I do not exist."

"Why do you feel that way? That was an interesting choice of words, referring to yourself as a non-entity."

"Because there is nothing in my life that stimulates me or gives me any pleasure anymore. I hate leaving the house, I hate getting dressed, I hate watching television, I have no desire to go back to work, I do not like talking to people. There is no one left in this world who would care if I was living or dead."

"What about your father, do you think he would care about burying his son?"

"Eh. He would get over it. So would Barry and Michele, so would Lucy. Everyone would move on, they do not need me. No one needs me."

"Have you given any thought to maybe trying to date again?"

"Have you lost your mind? None whatsoever. Nobody is ever going to compare to Frannie, and I will constantly be comparing. They say that there is one person on the planet for everyone. I found mine, and I lost her. There is nobody else out there for me, and I do not want there to be anyway."

"When was the last time you saw your father?"

"This morning, I came from his house."

"Is that where you drank?"

"No, I had time to kill, so I stopped at a bar on my way over here."

"Why is it that you felt you needed to stop at a bar on your way to our session?"

"I did not feel that I needed to. I just wanted to, and I had some time to kill."

"Why not go to a book store or the mall and walk

around?"

"There are too many people there. I do not like being around large groups of people and I certainly do not like or want to interact with them."

"This seems like a fairly recent development, since when do you have a fear of large groups of people?"

"I did not say it was a fear, I just do not like it. You called it a fear."

"Fair enough."

"I finally tried one of those support groups that you have been pushing me towards. I do not feel like going into detail as I just did with my father, but it was a fucking disaster. I actually got kicked out for verbally abusing another person speaking. I got so angry at her story of her college-aged daughter overdosing on drugs that I could not help myself. That is all I want to talk about regarding the support group, it was a horrible idea to send me to one. Like I said earlier, I am a ghost. I do not exist, and should not be engaging in society."

"Have you gotten any more letters from Hannah?"

"Not since May. I wrote her back in June."

"What did she have to say?"

"Are you making fun of me?"

"Why would you ask me that?"

"Because you have never done anything but put that whole scenario down, let alone ask about them in a non-judgmental manner."

"Ok, well now I am. So indulge me."

"She is doing good. She is not in any pain, neither is Frannie. They get to sleep together every night. They get to play dress-up together, and have tea parties together, all the things I used to do with her." And with that last sentence, Kenneth began to cry. It had been a while since he had cried, and the tears flowed with no abandon.

"Do you still feel like this whole letter writing campaign is a good idea?" Dr. Kaplan asked as he handed Kenneth a box of tissues.

"IT WAS YOUR FUCKING IDEA."

"There is no need to yell Kenneth. And the only part of the situation that was my suggestion was to write the letters; I never suggested that you mail them and I certainly never suggested that you engage in a fictitious pen pal ship with your deceased daughter."

"There is nothing fictitious about my daughter or the relationship that I have been able to continue with her."

The two of them sat in silence for several minutes. Dr. Kaplan felt that they had reached a bit of a crossroad. Kenneth's progress had markedly declined since he had last seen him; apparently declining inversely to his blossoming drinking habit. He believed Kenneth to be an alcoholic, one who was also suffering from depression and paranoid delusions. He had no way, no easy way, to communicate to Kenneth that the letters were not actually coming from Hannah. He just did not want to hear it, let alone believe it. If Dr. Kaplan said the wrong thing, there is no telling how Kenneth would react.

"How long do you plan on writing and mailing letters to Hannah?"

"Forever. Or at least for as long as she keeps responding."

"That is a very big concern of mine. What is going to happen if and when "she" stops responding?"

"I have never given that any thought."

"Perhaps you should. It is a little unrealistic to think that you are just going to continue receiving letters from her for the remainder of your life."

"Are we about done here?" Kenneth asked, his voice filled with annoyance.

"You cannot keep running away from me anytime I say or ask something you do not like. And the answers to your problems do not lie at the bottom of a bottle of bourbon."

"And we are done." Kenneth got up, paid Dr. Kaplan his $30 co-pay, and made for the exit.

"What you are doing right now is classic avoidance behavior. You cannot keep running Kenneth, the problems will continue to catch up to you if you do not deal with them." Dr. Kaplan said to Kenneth's back as Kenneth headed for the exit. "I am worried about you."

"Goodbye Dr. Kaplan."

CHAPTER XXVIII

A few days later, Kenneth arrived home from the liquor store to find that he had a letter from Hannah. This was a quicker turnaround than usual, one that filled Kenneth with an excitement he had not felt since the last letter arrived. He poured himself a glass of bourbon and excitedly took the letter into the living room.

June 19, 2015

Dear Daddy,

Is everything ok? Your last letter to me was very short and it seemed like you were sad. That made me a little upset, I have told you before, I do not want you to be sad. I am happy that you apologized to Ricky, he is your best friend and you need him. That is what you always told me, and Ricky was always super nice to me.

I like to draw pretty pictures of princesses for Mommy and I also like to make paintings for her. There is a big wall here that Mommy always hangs my artwork on, just like my Wall of Fame back at the house. She tells me she is very proud of the work I do, especially since she left us when I was really young and never got to see any of my artwork. I also draw a lot of pictures of the family, she says they are really good. She calls them portraits, but I am not really sure what that means.

I am SO SO happy you went to see Poppy, I miss him a lot. I used to have so much fun with him, especially when he took me fishing. I thought it was so funny picking up the worms and them wiping my hands on Poppy's jeans. Maybe sometime Poppy can write me a letter too? Poppy was always so nice to me, I loved playing with him.

This also will be a short letter, I really just wanted to make sure you were ok. I imagine you being sad and it made me sad. I want you to be happy. I love and miss you lots.

Your Princess,
Hannah

Before she had written this letter, Jennifer had thought long and hard about what to say. For starters, Kenneth had not given her much to work with in his latest letter. Further, his last letter came off sounding a bit on the depressive side. She was unsure what was causing the sudden shift in his demeanor, and could only hope that she was not playing a role in that. Her intentions were nothing but positive.

This whole "relationship" she had developed with Kenneth had certainly been a positive experience for her. She was starting to feel more confident in social interactions with others, even engaging somewhat in daily conversations with co-worker Sam. She was still intimidated by Louis and chose not to engage him in conversation outside of a perfunctory "hello, how are you?" She still had not shared her actions with Louis, only Sam, knowing that do so would land her in a lot of hot water.

Jennifer still viewed her actions as harmless. The letters that Kenneth wrote would otherwise have been returned as undeliverable, so it was not as if someone was missing out on mail that they should have received. She actually thought she was helping Kenneth, perhaps giving him some hope where previously there was none. She would love to meet him in person someday, but she knew that was out of the question. He just seemed like a good man to her, and certainly a loving father. A loving father who was lost and looking for answers. This was unsurprising given the manner in which he had lost Hannah.

Although she could not communicate with him directly, she did however park outside his home on a few occasions, on the other side of the street of course. She had to know what he looked like, to at least put a visual to the person she had been exchanging the most personal of letters with. After finally seeing him, the best way she could describe him was disheveled. He did not look like he shaved often, and frequently left the house in nothing other than sweat pants and a tee shirt. She was unsure if he was employed, and if so, in what capacity. He did not appear to leave the house often.

On several occasions, she felt and fought off the urge to approach him. There simply would be no gain to anyone if she did that. So she remained content just viewing him from a distance. He seemed like a very melancholy man, which was justifiable given what he had been through. She just wished that she could do more.

CHAPTER XXIX

Kenneth sat stoically in Dr. Kaplan's office, not feeling very well about himself or the way the last meeting had ended.

"I am sorry for walking out of our last meeting, I do not know why I did that."

"You do not have to apologize to me, it is your dime." Dr. Kaplan responded with a chuckle, trying to lighten the mood a bit. "Besides, you walking out is becoming something of a habit, I am used to it and do not take it personally. I told you last time why you walked out, it was called avoidance behavior. You did not like what we were talking about, or rather what I had to say about it, so you left. It was classic avoidance behavior, nothing more, nothing less. But as we talked about, avoiding the problem is not going to make the problem go away. Not to say that talking about them will make them go away either, but it will make them easier to manage as we go along. Before we start, I have to ask, did you have anything to drink before our session today?"

"No."

"Good. Then I get a clear-headed Kenneth for once."

"I understand what you are saying about the avoidance behavior. However, it does not seem like anything is getting any easier. I wake up with the same heartache, the same pain, the same emptiness. Do you know what it is like to wake up feeling incomplete? It is a horrible feeling. I made myself a promise that I would not drink before noon, so I find myself sitting and watching the clock until I can have that drink. That and the letters from Hannah are the only things that are keeping me going."

"You realize of course, that both of those things that "keep you going" are serious problem behaviors, don't you?"

"I do not see it that way, I see them as lifelines."

"You need to go to AA Kenneth, you have all the telltale signs of alcoholism. You think about drinking all the time, you drink by yourself, you drink a lot, and your sole thought process is when during the day it is acceptable for you to start drinking. You also vehemently deny that you have a drinking problem."

"I just do not see it as a problem, it helps me get through the day. It is an escape from my hell."

"That sentence, in and of itself, belies the problem. You cannot get through the day without alcohol. That is textbook alcoholism. You need help that I am not trained to provide."

"Noted."

"Do you feel ready to rationally discuss the letters to and from Hannah yet?"

"What is there to discuss?"

"The fact that they are not coming from Hannah, the fact that she is deceased."

"Everyone keeps saying that. I know that she is deceased. Nobody knows that more than me. But there is a higher power at play here, something other-worldly for lack of a better word that I cannot explain. The letters are coming from Hannah, and you are not going to convince me otherwise."

"Ok then, we can discuss something else. Why is it that you feel so incomplete? You are still here, you are still a person. You still have a lot to offer the world. I know that I have asked before, but when, if at all, do you plan on returning to work?"

"I am not going to return to work."

"Why not?"

"Several reasons. I have absolutely no desire to go back

to work. I just cannot bring myself to care. Working in litigation requires a lot of effort in getting to know your client, leaning about its business if it is a corporate client, a tremendous amount of communication with the client and their insurance companies – none of which I have any desire to do. Plus, as a Senior Associate, my only reward for doing good work is receiving more work. Even if I did care about those things, there is absolutely no incentive to doing them well. Being made Partner is out of the question because I have no "book of business," nor do I have any interest in going off to build one. So as you can see, going back to my position would bring nothing positive to my life other than money, which I also no longer care about or am in need of."

"But you are still receiving a salary from them, are you not? Does that not seem like you are taking advantage of them a bit?"

"They can afford it."

"What about doing something outside of the legal field?"

"That is not such an easy transition. People always say that there is "so much you can do with a law degree." I challenge those people to identify some of those things. They do not exist. My skillset is very narrow and defined. And talk about not caring about things, learning a new profession from the ground up is pretty low on the list of things I can or want to do at this stage of my life. I simply have no interest in being employed in any capacity."

"So what is your plan?"

"My plan is to keep living off of my savings, Frannie's life insurance money, and my salary for as long as they will continue to pay it. I also plan to continue receiving my monthly phone call from the firm's HR department asking about my health and projected return date, while I recover from my "shock."

"You know good and well that the firm's good will and phone calls are not going to last forever."

"I have no expectation that it will last forever, or much longer for that matter. It is funny that my monthly phone calls come from HR and not from an actual Partner. Partners cannot bill anyone for such a phone call. I tell HR that I am still suffering tremendously, and they say ok and tell me to take my time."

"Again, it sounds like you are taking advantage a little bit of the firm's generosity."

"I do not look at it that way. They worked my ass into the ground with zero reward, I deserve what I am getting now. I earned it. And besides, I never lie to them. When I tell them I am suffering tremendously, that is not a lie. You cannot deny that."

"I would agree that you are suffering. I do not agree that continuing to lead the firm on, knowing that you are not going back and still collecting a salary, is an honest or ethical thing to do."

"You know me pretty well by now. Do you honestly think I care about the ethics of the situation?"

"Honesty and ethical behavior are things that should be important, they help forge a person's core. Are they not qualities that you would try you instill in your daughter if she were still here?"

"I suppose there is an argument there. But she is not here anymore, and I am not looking to "forge my core" as you put it. I am simply loafing my way through life, wallowing between pain and misery, one day at a time. It is taking forever."

"What is taking forever?"

"Life is."

"That is a horrible outlook on life, Kenneth."

"You go through all that I have been through and see

how cheery and optimistic you can be."

"Nobody is asking you to be cheerful. I am simply asking you to put forth some effort to work with me to improve your outlook on things."

"I feel like we are going in circles. How many times can I tell you that I do not want my outlook to improve. I do not want to feel better. I do not want to "improve" because doing so would require that I let go of Hannah, and I am not going to do that."

"You are stuck in a rut, and you are spiraling downwards, fast."

"Well that may be true, but I do not see anything that can be done about that. Things are the way they are."

"Our time is up for today. I am giving you a list of local AA groups. I am urging you, pleading with you, to attend a group and try to get some help for your problem."

Kenneth paid his copay and threw the AA list in the

garbage pail in Dr. Kaplan's lobby.

CHAPTER XXX

A few weeks went by as Kenneth's living conditions continued to deteriorate. He stopped caring about his physical appearance altogether, he stopped shaving, and his drinking habit and Klonopin intake were taking on a life of their own. He stopped leaving the house, missing several appointments with Dr. Kaplan, and simply spent his days agonizing over the loss of Hannah. It was his turn, so to speak, to write Hannah back. He had been hesitant to do so because he just had nothing even remotely upbeat to share with her. After much consideration, he decided to write her anyway. He was four glasses of bourbon and two Klonopins in when he made that decision.

July 11, 2015

Dear Princess Hannah,

Thank you for your last letter. You were right in that I am very sad. I love getting letters from you, it is the only thing that keeps me going, the only thing that brings a smile to my face. Hearing about the time you get to spend with Mommy warms my heart. She left us when you were so young so you never really got to know her very well.

Let me tell you a little about Mommy, stuff you may not know. Mommy was the most caring person I had ever met, with the biggest heart. She taught me how to care, and she taught me how to love. Before I met her, I was not a complete person because I did not know how to love. I became a better person because of her.

There was a time I remember that Mommy and me were walking through the city, that is where your Uncle Barry and Aunt Michele lived at the time, and a man came up to us who had no home, no job, and no money. He asked us if we could give him some money because he had not eaten in a long time. My instant reaction was to say no and continue walking. However, Mommy approached the situation very differently. She told the man to wait where he was and that we would be right back. She took me by the hand into a deli that was nearby and ordered a turkey sandwich, bag of chips, and a hot cup of coffee. She took all the food she ordered and brought it back to the man on the street. He was very appreciative of the gesture and thanked Mommy over and over again.

This was just the kind of person that Mommy was, she genuinely cared for the well-being of others. She was a lovely person and she did not deserve to get so sick at such a young age. When she left me, I felt like she took a big piece of my heart with her. But I had to be strong for you, and I was.

I am very jealous of the time you get to spend with her now. I wish more than anything that I could be there with you two, so that we could be a family again. I know and feel in my heart that we will be reunited again soon.

I had a very nice visit with Poppy, he misses you a lot. We talked a lot about you, and the fun memories he has of taking you fishing. He said that some of his jeans still have stains on them from the worm guts you wiped on him!

Everyone misses you, but none more than me Princess. It used to warm my heart when you smiled. And when you used to laugh, it was so contagious that it would make everyone in the room laugh. I long to hear that laugh again.

I love you with all my heart.

Love,
Daddy

CHAPTER XXXI

Kenneth was sitting in his living room when the doorbell rang, a little after 1:00 pm. He was not expecting any visitors so he ignored it. About one minute later, it rang again. Heading to the front door, Kenneth angrily yelled that he was not interested in buying anything.

"Not even from your best friend?" Asked a voice from the other side of the door that was unmistakably Ricky's. Kenneth unlocked and opened the door, and then walked back into the living room where his bourbon was. Ricky let himself in and followed Kenneth, who was still in sweat pants and a tee shirt, into the living room.

"Kenneth, you absolutely reek of alcohol."

"So fucking what, is that what you came over here to tell me?"

"Jules and I are worried about you. I suspect you have not been out of the house for a while. You have obviously stopped shaving, have you even been showering?"

"Yes mom. You want to know what I do in the shower? I cry. Hysterically. I also turn the water up all the way, as hot as it goes, the physical pain sometimes helps me forget the emotional pain. Sometimes, but not always. What else do you want to know?"

"Do you eat? Or do you exist solely on a diet comprised of bourbon and pills?"

"I eat sometimes." Kenneth was a bit surprised, he did not realize anyone was aware of the vast quantities of pills he had been taking. He was somewhat curious how Ricky knew, but did not care enough to ask.

"Really? Because not only do you look like a slovenly

alcoholic and drug addict, you also look like you have lost a

ton of weight. I will ask again, are you eating?"

"I just answered that question, I eat sometimes."

"You are wasting away Kenneth. Can you not see that?"

"I can, I simply do not care."

"You know there are still people here who care about

you and depend on you, right?"

"Such as?"

"Jules and I for starters. I have been your best friend for

years. Jules has cared about you since her and I met, even

before we were married. And what about your father, siblings,

and niece and nephew? Who is going to tell your father that

he is going to have to bury his son if you keep on this path? It

sure as hell is not going to be me."

"You just named a bunch of people who may care about

me, but there is certainly nobody on that list who depends on

me. My father would be fine. He has had plenty of losses in

his lifetime and always bounced back fine, this would be no different."

"Listen, there is an AA meeting tomorrow night right here in Brighton. I will go with you."

"I do not need an AA meeting. If I wanted to stop drinking, I would. I just have absolutely no desire to stop. It makes the days less hellish."

"Are you still corresponding with your deceased daughter?" Kenneth picking up a hint of sarcasm in Ricky's voice.

"That is what is keeping me alive."

"That is what is scaring us the most. Not the booze, not the pills. Especially now that you are telling me that is the sole thing keeping you alive. Do you hear yourself?"

"Ricky, can we be done here?"

"Can I trust that you will be safe if I leave you alone?"

"I do not care what you trust to be honest. I am not

your child."

"Then I guess we are done here. You know, we used to spend hours on end together, watching football, shooting the shit, you were never so short with me. Why won't you talk to me anymore? Did I do something to piss you off?"

"No, it is just that the landscape has changed, wouldn't you agree?"

"Yes, the landscape may have changed a bit, but that does not mean you have to shut out the people who care about you. Let us, or at least let me, be your support system. I want to help you, let me help you. You are not going to get through this with alcohol and pills as your best friends."

"It is too late, Ricky. I hear you, I understand what you are saying, I just do not want the help. It is nothing personal, you did not do anything wrong. I have said it a million times already, I am not willing to put Hannah behind me. That is what it will take in order to move on and "get better." That is how I feel and it is not going to change. There is nothing anyone can do or say that is going to change that because in my heart, that is not going to change. I will not let her go."

"I am sure your doctor has said this to you, but you can heal without letting her go, you do not have to forget her to heal."

"Enough. I do not want to hear it from him, and I do not want to hear it from you. If you do not mind, I would like to be alone now. Thank you for coming over."

"Ok Ken, just remember what I said. I know I am going out on a limb here, but maybe you can come over to the house one of these days for dinner? You need to eat. Jules and the kids would love to see you."

"To be perfectly frank, that is not going to happen. I just cannot bring myself to go out for anything other than booze or food, the former more than the latter. And seeing people is even less desirable to me. Thank you for the offer though.

Goodbye Ricky."

"Ok, just keep it in mind, do not shut yourself in. I will leave you alone now. Be good buddy, I love you." Ricky hugged Kenneth goodbye and let himself out of the house. Kenneth went and poured himself another drink, took another Klonopin, and went to lay down in the living room, this being his plan for the remainder of the day.

CHAPTER XXXII

On opposite sides of town, both Jennifer and Ricky were feeling really sad for Kenneth. Jennifer read Kenneth's letter and could not help but feel saddened by how hard a time Kenneth seemed to be having at adapting to life without Hannah. She felt worried for him, even questioning some of his chosen words. She was particularly concerned when he said he could not wait to be with Hannah and Frannie again. This was the first time that she had an inkling of a thought that maybe her letters were doing more harm than good. However, now that she had initiated and engaged this relationship, she did not know if she could stop. Or if it was even prudent to stop. She had seen, especially by way of his latest letter, just how dependent he had become on the letters she wrote him.

"He does not really believe the letters are coming from Hannah, does he?" Jennifer wondered out loud to herself. If so, she could see this ending very poorly, and not something that she would be able to stop anytime soon. She would have to continue writing *ad infinitum*. From a purely selfish standpoint, she herself got a lot of benefit out of the pen pal ship, mainly that she was finally able to make a friend. Granted, she could not express any of her own emotions, needs, or wants, everything had to be from the perspective of a deceased, five year old girl whom she had never known. This was a difficult task, but one that she took on herself. Unfortunately, this was a predicament that she did not know how to handle and one for which she could not seek advice from anyone without landing herself in hot water. She was not used to feeling this type of confusion, which is why she typically kept everything in her life black-and-white. She thought to herself that if all types of relationships brought on these types of feelings, she was glad that she had all but avoided forging other relationships of her own.

On the other side of town, Ricky sat at his kitchen table talking to his wife Jules about Kenneth.

"I am so worried about him Jules." Ricky lamented.

"I know you are sweetheart. How did it go seeing him today?"

"It was depressing. He has really let himself go. He has stopped shaving, it did not look like he had changed his clothes in days, and he very clearly has a drug and alcohol problem. He reeked of alcohol."

"Did you say anything about the drinking to him today?"

"I told him that he was not going to get better sitting in the house all day drinking bourbon and popping pills."

"What was his response?"

"He did not really have one, he does not seem to think or care about whether or not he has a drinking problem."

"So what did you two talk about?"

"Hannah. He expressed to me that he does not want to get better, that he does not want to heal because he has this notion that in order for him to get better, he will have to forget Hannah or put her out of his mind. I tried to explain to him that healing and continuing to keep Hannah's legacy alive are not mutually exclusive, and that he can improve or rehabilitate while continuing to honor her."

"And what was his response to that? Was he receptive at all to what you had to say?"

"No. He really did not want to hear or believe anything I had to say. I am telling you Jules, he is like a completely different person from the man who has been my best friend for the past twenty-five years. I do not recognize him at all. He is an alcoholic. He is a drug addict. He is out of his mind, literally. He is obsessed with Hannah and those ridiculous letters he receives from "her."

"Have you considered going straight to the source?"

"What do you mean?"

"As you have explained it to me, he is writing letters to Hannah and "mailing" them to her, to an address in Heaven. Someone is writing back to him, which has to be someone from the post office. This is not New York City, the post office cannot have too many people working there, so it should not be too hard to figure out who the mystery author is. Once you figure that out, you should be able to put a stop to it. Then Kenneth will be able to start an honest and legitimate healing process."

"That is a good idea Jules, I am going to go down there tomorrow and talk to the Manager. Thanks sweetheart, I am glad we had this discussion."

"Anytime. You will get my bill in the mail."

"I just want my friend back, I would pay anything for that."

CHAPTER XXXIII

There was only one post office in Brighton, so that part was easy. It was actually close to Ricky's house, so he chose to walk over since it was such a nice day out. He arrived at the post office a little after 10:00 am so that he could talk to the Manager before the lunch crowd came in. Upon his arrival, he was greeted by a pleasant African-American man who appeared to be in his late 50s. Ricky approached the man, introduced himself, and asked if he could speak to the Manager.

"My name is Louis and I am the Branch Manager, how may I help you?" Responded Louis in a very friendly and courteous manner.

"May I have a few minutes of your time, in private, it is a bit of a sensitive matter."

"Of course. Sam, come here please." Sam came out from the back asking "what's up boss?"

"I need you to man the front desk while I speak with this gentleman in my office for a few minutes."

"No problem boss." Sam replied.

Ricky followed Louis into a small office near the back of the building. The office was decorated with an array of, what Ricky could only describe, as post office memorabilia. For example, there was a giant poster commemorating different celebrity stamps through the years. There was also a large chart illustrating the meteoric rise in stamp prices over the years.

"You will have to excuse the decor," Louis said sheepishly, "I am a bit of a mail junkie. That is what happens when you work in a post office for thirty-four years. My wife will not let me hang any of this "junk" in the house, so here it goes. Well I am sure you did not come here to discuss my love of stamps, what is it that I can help you with sir?"

"I need to give you a bit of background before I explain how you can help me." Ricky began. "My best friend, a man named Kenneth Hill, has had a tumultuous few years, to say the least. First, he lost his wife to cancer approximately five years ago. He and his wife had a one year old daughter at the time, whom Kenneth was left to raise all by himself.

Tragically," Ricky continued, "four years later, his then five year old daughter was killed when the car she and Kenneth were traveling in was hit by a drunk driver."

"I think I remember reading about this in the papers." Louis chimed in.

"Very likely, it was the top story on an otherwise slow news day. Anyway, Kenneth's therapist recommended that he write letters to his daughter, Hannah, as a therapeutic exercise to aid in the grieving process. Kenneth did this, but unfortunately, took it one step further. He took the letters he wrote and began to mail them to Hannah in "Heaven."

"We get lots of letters like that every year. Santa Claus, God, and the Easter Bunny are particularly popular." Louis interjected. "Such letters, as a matter of post office policy, are returned to the sender marked undeliverable."

"If that had been the end of the story, I would not be sitting here Louis. Much to the surprise and pleasure of Kenneth and the chagrin of nearly everyone around him, Kenneth started receiving letters back from "Hannah." Kenneth is a very sick individual, you see, and he has come to believe that he is actually receiving letters from his deceased daughter. There is absolutely no talking sense into him, and this has been a significant causal factor in his going off the proverbial deep end. As his best friend for more than two decades, this has been very difficult to witness.

What I am asking of you sir should be very simple. I do not imagine that you have a very sizeable staff here. I am asking that you find the person who is receiving and responding to Kenneth's letters and put a stop to it."

"First off, I am very sorry to hear about your friend, this is an incredibly heart wrenching story. No man should ever have to bury his child, that is not how life is supposed to unfold. I have two children, and I could not bear the thought of having to put either of them in the ground.

I can assure you that if one of my employees is in fact taking your friend's letters and responding to them, I will put a stop to it immediately and ensure that that person is disciplined and dealt with appropriately."

"I cannot thank you enough for being so receptive to my concerns and my request. As you can imagine, this is a very tough situation for all involved, worst of all for Kenneth. I appreciate your help, I will not use up any more of your time."

"Have a good day sir, you have my word that this will be dealt with immediately." They parted ways at the front entrance and Louis went back into his office to process what had just occurred. He was furious, if what this man said was true, such an action would be the most flagrant violation of his policies that he had ever witnessed in his thirty-four year career. He was determined to deal with this person, which could only be one of two people, and to deal with them immediately.

Ricky, on the other hand, left the post office feeling good about his meeting with Louis, and feeling confident that this situation would be dealt with in a manner that would benefit Kenneth. Things were looking up he told himself.

CHAPTER XXXIV

Jennifer awoke Thursday morning feeling a lit bit
groggy having not had a great night's sleep. She had been
somewhat out of it ever since she received Kenneth's latest
letter. The letter had been dripping with his grief, and she felt
completely helpless. The tone of his letters had taken a
definite downturn over the past few months and she wished
there was something she could do to help him.

She showered and got ready for work, following her
usual routine to a "T." At least it was a nice day out so she
somewhat enjoyed her walk to the post office. She was greeted
upon her arrival by Louis in a most unusual manner, with his
asking her to come into his office. She also noticed that Sam

was sorting the incoming mail, not his usual task but rather that was Jennifer's job. She knew something was amiss.

Louis asked Jennifer to take a seat in his office as he closed the door behind her. He seemed more stern than usual.

"Jennifer," Louis began, "I received some very disturbing news yesterday." Louis was very direct and not one to beat around the bush. "A man came into the post office to tell me that his best friend, who lost his daughter at a very young age, has been writing letters to the deceased girl, addressed to her in Heaven. That is not the disturbing part, as you know we get many types of these letters year round. What is disturbing is that instead of marking the letters "undeliverable" and returning them to the sender, someone has been taking the letters out of the post office and taking it upon themself to actually write letters back to the sender. This has happened on numerous occasions, with all the letters coming from the deceased girl. I asked Sam and he did not know anything about this. Now I will ask you the same question, do you know anything about this Jennifer?"

Jennifer remained silent for a minute, looking down at the floor. Then, totally uncontrolled and out of character for her, she began to sob.

"I was only trying to help him. I thought that if he got letters back from his daughter, it would make his recovery a little bit easier."

Louis was stunned. "There are several problems with that, Jennifer. I am shocked at you. First, you are well aware that it is a violation of federal law to open other people's mail, as well as strict post office regulations that you have worked here long enough to know. Second, and putting all laws and regulations aside, from what I understand from the person who brought this to my attention, the letters have not been particularly helpful; instead, they have caused the sender to transition into somewhat of a psychotic state where he thinks the letters are actually coming from his deceased daughter!"

This last sentence made Jennifer cringe, as she honestly thought she was helping him. She continued to cry as Louis spoke.

"I am a bit torn," Louis continued, "I have known you for a very long time. You have always been a good employee and a very pleasant person to have around. I gave this a lot of thought. First, I am not going to involve the authorities at all with regard to your opening the mail. You are too good of a person to be in prison. However, I have to let you go. What you did violated the fundamental rules of this establishment, and there is no way that I can keep you on as an employee. There is simply no trust there anymore, you destroyed that.

This is a very difficult decision for me since I do like you so much and you have been here for so long and always have been a good employee. But you have left me with no choice. Your termination is effective immediately, you will receive your final pay check in the mail. If you have something underneath, I will need you to turn in your postal employee shirt. If not, please return the shirt to me within three days, as it is government property. Do you understand everything I have said?"

In between sobs, Jennifer indicated that she understood and apologized to Louis.

"Ok," Louis finished, "If there is nothing else, I need you to leave the premises immediately. Take care of yourself Jennifer."

And with that, Jennifer took off the postal employee shirt and handed it to Louis, having another shirt underneath. She then walked out of Louis' office, waved goodbye to Sam, and walked out of the post office for the final time.

CHAPTER XXXV

Jennifer arrived home about ten minutes later, dropping her bag on the living room table and sitting down on the couch to process everything that had just occurred. She cried, and could not recall the last time she cried so much. She was not certain if she was more upset over losing her job or the fact that her correspondence with Kenneth was going to have to come to an end. She loved her job because it was consistent, no one bothered her there, and it paid well-enough for her to maintain her apartment and live out of her mother's grasp. On the other hand, she highly valued the relationship she had developed with Kenneth, even if he was unaware of it.

She re-read his last letter, which only made her cry more. The letter was so depressing, Kenneth apparently stopped trying to hide his utter grief and expressed just how much he missed Hannah and how his life had deteriorated since her passing. She was unconvinced by what Louis had said about the letters to Kenneth doing more damage than good. She tried to put herself in Kenneth's shoes, which was not easy as she had never been a parent; however, she imagined that she would feel some sort of reprieve to receive letters from a child or loved one who passed. Based on this line of thinking, she made the conscious decision to write Kenneth one final, brief letter explaining that there would be no further letters. He deserved closure rather than an unexplained disappearance, or so Jennifer thought. So she got out her pad of paper and began to write.

August 4, 2015

Dear Daddy,

I received your last letter, you sound so sad Daddy. I know how hard I must be with me and Mommy gone. We miss you a lot also, but Mommy says you have to be strong. I agree with her, you have to be strong for yourself and for me and Mommy. And you have to know how much we love you.

This is a very hard letter to write because I have some bad news. The people here said that I am not allowed to write you any more letters. They said that the letters are probably causing you more pain than joy. They also said that by me sending you letters, I am interfering with your healing process. I had to ask Mommy what that meant, and she explained to me that my letters are stopping you from getting better. I did not understand this, I thought my letters would cheer you up. I thought you would be happy getting letters from me since you cannot see me anymore.

Me and Mommy tried to explain this to the people in

charge, but we could not convince them to let us write you

any more letters. So this is going to be the very last letter I

write to you. It makes me feel a little better that at least I get a

chance to say goodbye to you this time. The last time I left you

I did not even get a chance to say goodbye. I am sorry that this

has to end. I hope you are ok. I want you to be happy and I

want you to enjoy your life. We will be together again

someday, but not just yet. I love you Daddy. I will ALWAYS

be your Princess.

Love,
Hannah

Jennifer felt an unbridled sadness writing this letter, it

felt like a part of her soul was ripped out. She put a stamp on

the letter and walked it to the mailbox nearest to her house.

She thought of Sam sorting the letter tomorrow morning, and

got even more upset knowing that this was no longer her job.

She walked home, taking the longer, more scenic route to try and ease her mind. She arrived home, got ready for bed, and

cried herself to sleep.

CHAPTER XXXVI

It was two days later that Kenneth received Hannah's final letter. The day had not been a particularly good one, Kenneth had been drinking steadily for three hours when the letter arrived. He was not yet dressed or showered, and he could not recall the last time that he ate. He perked up quite a bit when he finally took in the day's mail and saw that he had a letter from Hannah. He had no idea what was about to hit him.

Kenneth took his bourbon and the letter into the living room, sitting down to see what his Princess had to say. He anxiously opened the letter and read it in its entirety. At first, he thought it was some kind of joke. So he read it two more times until the message clearly sank in. He launched his glass of bourbon against the living room wall, glass shattering in every direction, the wall being soaked with alcohol. Kenneth fell to his knees, looked upwards, and screamed: "How much more can you take from me? This cannot be true, what did I do to deserve this? What I ask you? If you were looking for my breaking point, you fucking found it."

Refusing to believe that life and karma could be so unforgiving, he immediately sat down with pen and paper, ignoring the shards of glass that were scattered all around him. He clumsily picked up the pen and began writing.

August 6, 2015

Dear Princess Hannah,

I received your most recent letter, it made me extremely sad. I do not understand why you cannot write me any more letters. I never said that they were hurting me in any way. It was the complete opposite, Princess, your letters brought me joy and happiness. I do not want to stop receiving letters from you, I simply cannot. Please please please keep writing me. I beg of you. I love and miss you, Princess.

Love,
Daddy

Kenneth put a stamp on the letter and addressed the letter to Hannah Hill, Heaven, and mailed it just as he always did. Each day thereafter, he waited for the postal worker at the door, akin to a child waiting for Santa Claus the night before Christmas. He did not have to wait long for a response. Three days after mailing his letter, it was returned to him with a bright red stamp on the front that read "Undeliverable: Address Unknown."

Kenneth took the letter inside and collapsed on the floor, whimpering as he read the message over and over again. "No, no, no" he shouted to no one in particular. This had to be a mistake. All of his previous letters had been delivered, there was no reason for this one to be any different. Stubbornly, he tried again. He opened the envelope, put the letter in a new one, addressed it to Hannah Hill, Heaven, put a stamp on it, and walked it to the nearest mailbox. Three days letter, it again came back to him with the same "Undeliverable: Address Unknown" stamp on it.

Accepting that all communication with his daughter had come to an end, he knew what his next course of action had to be. It was time he was reunited with Frannie and Hannah.

CHAPTER XXXVII

"Anything worth doing is worth doing right" Kenneth said to himself as he sat on the living room couch making his final preparations. He did not want to be labeled as someone who made a failed suicide attempt. Kenneth felt that was either a concession of failure or desperate plea for attention, neither of which he wanted to be tagged with.

His first order of business was to go to the pharmacy and buy a box of sleeping pills. He was amused that he had to show his ID to buy them, not realizing that sleeping pills were abused nowadays to the point that they became age-restricted. Having proven he was old enough to vote, he bought the box of sleeping pills and went home.

Next up on his list, apart from the bourbon and Klonopin, was his goodbye letters. He made a mental list of who had to get one. He decided on his father, his brother and sister, and Ricky. However, the prospect of writing so many separate letters seemed far too daunting a task for him and his alcohol-addled mind. He concluded that he would write one letter to all of them, essentially killing several birds with one stone. He took out the pad of paper he used to write Hannah on, and wrote the following:

August 15, 2015

Dear Pop, Lucy, Barry, Michele, and Ricky,

On first glance, it may seem disrespectful that I wrote one collective letter to the five of you in lieu of individual letters. Do not be offended, it was not meant this way. It was done simply as a matter of convenience, as the general sentiment and reasons behind my decision to take my own life are the same, regardless of the addressee.

Pop – you always said to us growing up that your favorite phrase was "this too shall pass." For most of my life, I believed this to be true. Then Frannie died, and I tried to apply that motto and set out to be the best father a man could be. And then, mercilessly, my Princess Hannah was taken away from me all because a drunk man decided he was able to drive home.

Hannah's passing is the defining moment of my life. Burying one's own child should never be the defining moment of a person's life, that presents a grief that is too unbearable to process. Since losing Hannah, I have not been myself, I know that. I have lost all faith in humanity and the common decency of mankind. I can no longer look my fellow man in the eye. Some may argue that this makes me less of a man, and this is a sentiment I cannot entirely disagree with. I am less of a man, less of a person. This is simply not a society that I want to continue to be a part of, and it is apparently not a society that wants me back. If it was, it would not keep taking things from me.

I do not want you to think that this was an action that was hastily decided upon, and certainly not one that was taken lightly. I thought about this long and hard. It is my only option to rid myself of the pain, the guilt, the anger, the frustration, the utter sting of despair. It is my only option to heal. To be reunited with Frannie and Hannah is the only way that I can become whole again. I am sorry, but there is simply no other way.

I will miss each one of you dearly in my own special way. I know how hard each of you tried to "get me out of my funk" and bring me back to life. I truly appreciate the efforts, and I am sorry if you feel like I failed you. Take solace in knowing you did all you could, but in the end, no amount of effort in the world was going to bring me back.

I love you all. Do not mourn my loss. Be happy for me that I will finally be reunited with my girls. I wish you all nothing but health and happiness going forward. If you all want to do me one last favor, hug your kids a little tighter today. Tell them you love them and really mean it.

Goodbye for now.

Love,
Kenneth

Kenneth finished his letter, put it in an envelope, and placed the envelope on the kitchen counter. On the front, he wrote: "to be read by Dad, Barry, Michele, Lucy, and Ricky." He then went upstairs to shave and shower, Hannah loved when he was clean shaven. He wanted to look his best for his girls. He then put on his finest suit and shoes, the ones Hannah always told him he looked handsome in.

He then went downstairs and took a few final swigs of bourbon, using the alcohol to swallow approximately ten of

the sleeping pills. He then proceeded to the garage. Once inside the garage, he ensured that all the doors, including the garage door, were tightly closed. He got into the driver's seat of his car and taped a picture of Hannah to the steering wheel. Her beautiful smile was the last thing he wanted to see.

As he began to feel the sleeping pills kick in, he started the car. He took one last look at Hannah's picture, and said: "Here comes my chariot, I am on my way Princess." And with that, off he went...

EPILOGUE

It had been nearly a week since Kenneth's body had been found by Barry. Notwithstanding Kenneth's pleas to the otherwise, they could not be happy for him. They could only mourn him. Mourn his life. Mourn his promise. Mourn his downfall. Mourn his death.

As he was walking in, Barry noticed the mailbox had not been emptied in a few days. He emptied the box and threw the stack of mail down on the kitchen table. As executor of Kenneth's estate, he had no choice but to make Kenneth's affairs his own, not a task he relished.

After aimlessly wandering around Kenneth's house for a bit, Barry sat down at the kitchen table. As he looked at the stack of mail, he noticed a small, pink envelope sticking out.

He took it out and his mouth fell wide open, for what

appeared before him was a letter addressed to "Daddy," with

a return address of "Hannah Hill, Heaven."

ACKNOWLEDGEMENTS

"The miracle is not to walk on water. The miracle is to walk on the green earth in the present moment, to appreciate the peace and beauty that are available now." – Thich Nhat Hanh.

Sometimes our darkest paths lead to the brightest clearings, and my experience was no different. I would like to acknowledge several people, apart from my family and friends of course, who helped lead me to those clearings.

Thich Nhat Hahn, the astounding visionary of peace, teacher, and poet, whose words on the subject of mindfulness moved and guided me exponentially more than any predecessors. His teachings were where I began to realize the importance of living in the "here and now." Through his teachings, I started to see life very differently, and learned how to appreciate life, instead of fearing it. I wish Thay the speediest of recoveries so that he may continue touching the lives of millions.

To Silver Hill Hospital in New Canaan, Connecticut. While it was not always easy to see the "big picture," I can safely say now that going to Silver Hill saved my life. The folks there "took over" when everyone else had run out of ideas, myself included. It was at Silver Hill that I was introduced to mindfulness and dialectical behavioral therapy, both of which undoubtedly changed my life.

More importantly, it was at Silver Hill that I was introduced to some of the most supportive, intelligent, and caring people I have ever known. Though I am hesitant to name individuals on the staff for fear of forgetting anyone, I would be remiss if I did not specifically thank Denise Kearns,

Brad Bloom, and Kate of River House. Staff aside, I also met several incredibly inspiring, courageous, and brave residents who through "shared sufferings," I was able to form bonds with that I hope will last a lifetime. I will certainly not name names, but you know who you are.

To the team at CCDBT in Lake Success, particularly: Dr. Elizabeth Gellman, Dr. Mary Carnesale, Dr. Jessica Brodsky, and Dr. Adam Payne (http://ccdbt.com)... your efforts towards driving home and practicing those skills I learned at Silver Hill, while keeping the material fresh without breaking the continuity, is a thing to marvel. The role you have played in my recovery and success is immeasurable.

To Irene Karp of "Step Up To Health" (http://stepuptohealthny.com), whose tireless dedication and genuine concern for my well-being has consistently gone far above and beyond what is expected of a doctor-patient relationship. One of the reasons I never quit on myself was because she would not let me quit. She forced me to fight, and continues to do so. With her help, I am growing into a better husband, a better father, a better son, a better brother, a better friend... a better person.

Finally, to Allie Brosh (http://hyperboleandahalf.blogspot.com) and Jenny Lawson (http://thebloggess.com)... you showed me that laughter, or more importantly, making other people laugh, is still possible even when facing the darkest days.

To all of you... thank you.

ABOUT THE AUTHOR

Scott Eisenberg lives on Long Island with his wife of ten years, two young children, a dog named Cookie, and a fish named Raindrop. A graduate of the Maurice A. Deane School of Law at Hofstra University, he practices law as a general liability defense litigator for one of the most dynamic and fastest-growing law firms in the United States.

Eisenberg's own struggles with severe depression, like Tolstoy, Woolf, and Hemingway before him, guide his writing about mental illness as he tackles such difficult topics as addiction, substance abuse, depression, loss of loved ones, and self-harm.